Mr Twiddle Fetches Polly

and

Other Stories

by
ENID BLYTON

Illustrated by
Maggie Downer

AWARD PUBLICATIONS LIMITED

For further information on Enid Blyton please visit *www.blyton.com*

ISBN 978-1-84135-487-3

First published by Award Publications Limited 2003
This edition first published 2008

Published by Award Publications Limited,
The Old Riding School, The Welbeck Estate,
Worksop, Nottinghamshire, S80 3LR

12 4

Printed in the United Kingdom

CONTENTS

Mr Twiddle
Fetches Polly

"Twiddle, you're not listening to what I'm saying!" said Mrs Twiddle.

"Yes, I am, dear," said Twiddle, without looking up from his paper. "I like listening to you. You go on and on like a dear little brook, and—"

"Twiddle! A brook doesn't ask questions and I do!" said Mrs Twiddle. "Will you please answer what I've just asked you!"

"Oh – did you ask me something?" said Twiddle in surprise. "What was it?"

"Now, Twiddle – I've been telling you about Polly, who's living with Miss Pepper at Grey Roofs," said Mrs Twiddle.

"Oh, yes, yes – of course!" said Twiddle, who hadn't heard a word about Polly.

"And I told you I wanted you to go and fetch her and bring her here," said Mrs Twiddle. "I've said I'll let her stay with us for a day or two while Miss Pepper is away – now don't tell me you didn't hear a word!"

"I wouldn't dream of telling you anything of the sort!" said Twiddle. "Of course I'll fetch Polly. How old is she?"

"I've no idea," said Mrs Twiddle. "She won't be very big. She's got a lot to say for herself, Miss Pepper tells me, so it will be fun to have her here for a day or two. She's a proper chatterbox!"

Mr Twiddle quite forgot that he had to go and fetch Polly that morning, and Mrs Twiddle, who thought he had gone long since, was very cross when she saw him sitting in the garden. She put her head out of the window.

"Twiddle! There – you've forgotten to fetch Polly! I knew you would!"

"No, I haven't! I'm just going!" said Twiddle, and leaped to his feet. He hurried indoors to get his hat and stick.

"Now, you know where to go, don't

you?" called Mrs Twiddle. "I think I'd better write it down for you, Twiddle. Miss Pepper at Grey Roofs – now, where's my pencil?"

"I can remember a simple thing like that, thank you!" said Twiddle, and walked off in a huff. Good gracious, anyone would think he couldn't even go and call for a little girl called Polly without having it all written down for him! Really, Mrs Twiddle was treating him like a donkey!

He went off down the road, swinging

his stick crossly. But the sun was nice and warm, and he soon forgot to be cross. He went up the hill and made his way to a little lane. He came to a house with a name on the gate. Ha – Green Roofs – this was where Polly lived. Now he must go in and ask for Miss Pepper and get Polly. He went in and knocked at the door. A little maid answered it.

"Good morning," said Mr Twiddle, politely. "Is Miss Pepper at home?"

The little maid giggled. "You've made a mistake," she said. "It's Miss Salt that lives here, sir."

"Dear me – how stupid of me!" said Twiddle, thinking that he had mixed up pepper and salt. "I mean Miss Salt, of course."

"She's out, sir," said the little maid. "Can I give her a message?"

"Well – I've come to fetch Polly," said Twiddle. "Is she ready to come?"

"Oh yes!" said the girl. "Miss Salt has already said goodbye to her. She dotes on her, you know! You won't want her cage, will you sir?"

"Her cage?" said Twiddle, startled. "Does she have a cage?"

"Well, of course!" said the maid. "But she uses her perch most of the time. And she's such a talker, sir! My, I never knew such a chatterbox!"

"Er – well, I heard she had a lot to say for herself," said Twiddle, feeling very surprised. "But really ..."

"Hello, hello, hello!" called a bright voice from indoors. "Good morning, good afternoon, goodnight!"

"That's Polly," said the maid, giggling at Mr Twiddle's surprise. "I'll get her, sir. She'll sit on your shoulder all the way back. She's no trouble at all."

She disappeared and came back with a pretty grey parrot with a red tail, whose feathers rose at the sight of Twiddle.

"Where's your hanky?" said the parrot at once and Twiddle felt in his pocket.

"Oh, you don't need to take any notice of what Polly says, sir!" said the maid. "Why do you look so surprised?"

"Well – er – to tell you the truth I was expecting another kind of Polly," said Twiddle. "Made a mistake, of course. Somehow I didn't think it would be a Polly like this. Will she really sit on my shoulder?"

"Oh yes," said the maid and put the bird on to his shoulder. "She'll stay there till you get back, sir. She's as good as gold – but oh, such a chatterbox!"

Twiddle said goodbye to the maid and went, walking rather cautiously in case the parrot fell off. Polly had no intention of falling, however, and dug her claws

hard into Twiddle's coat.

"Hello, hello, hello!" said the parrot when they met old Mrs Trip. She was short-sighted and didn't see the parrot on Twiddle's shoulder. She was most surprised to be shouted at like that.

"Good morning, Mr Twiddle!" she said, and swept by.

"Goodbye-eee!" called the parrot, cheekily, and Twiddle felt really cross.

"Be quiet," he said, fiercely.

11

"Shut up!" said the parrot at once. Twiddle decided not to have any more conversation after that. Instead, he began to feel extremely cross with Mrs Twiddle for saying she would have someone else's polly-parrot for a few days. Oh, why hadn't he listened that morning when Mrs Twiddle was telling him all about it? Then he wouldn't have made such a silly mistake.

The parrot began to sing. "Hush-a-bye-baby, on the tree-top!" it sang, and Twiddle went red right to his ears. What a dreadful bird! Making everyone stare at him. He was very, very glad when at last he came to his own front-gate.

He took the parrot indoors and shut the door. He set the bird down in the sitting-room and called to his wife.

"I've brought Polly back! I've put her in the sitting-room!"

And with that he hurried out into the garden to sit down with his paper again. What a bird! Well, he wouldn't go indoors more than he could help while that bird was with them!

He saw the cat sitting comfortably in his deckchair and turned it out. "Look – you go and see who's in the sitting-room!" he said. The cat turned her back on him and stalked off to the kitchen window.

Twiddle had a moment of panic. Suppose the cat attacked the bird and killed it! Goodness, what a to-do there would be! He listened in fear.

A loud voice came from the house. "Hello, hello, hello! Puss, puss, puss! One, two, three, four, five, three cheers, hip, hip, hooray!"

And then the cat appeared again, leaping hurriedly out through the window and back into the garden, all its

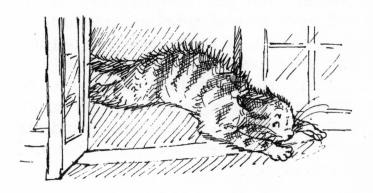

fur standing on end. What was that peculiar thing in the sitting-room?

Mrs Twiddle, upstairs in her bedroom, was rather surprised to hear the noise downstairs. She called from her bedroom door.

"I won't be a minute, Polly! Sit down, dear, and look at a book. I'm just changing my blouse."

"Hush-a-bye-baby, on the tree-top!" sang Polly, cheerfully.

"Dear little thing – singing nursery rhymes as good as gold," thought Mrs Twiddle. "It will be nice to have a child staying here for a day or two."

"Milko!" called Polly. "Milko! Coo-eeeee! All change, all change!" Then she whistled just like an express train.

Mrs Twiddle was rather shocked. Dear dear – to think a little girl could whistle like that! What would the neighbours say?

She went to the top of the stairs. "Be quiet, dear!" she called. "I'll soon be down. Be quiet, now!"

"Shut up!" said Polly, in glee. "Bang-

bang, you're dead! Pass the salt, please. Hip-hooray!"

"What an extraordinary child," thought Mrs Twiddle, anxiously. "I don't think Twiddle will like her – especially if she tells him to shut up. Most impolite."

"Good morning, good afternoon, good-night!" shouted Polly. "How-do-you-do, you'll miss your train, there it goes!" And she whistled again. Even Twiddle heard her out in the garden, and as for the cat, it shot right to the very back of the shed and hid there.

Mrs Twiddle hurried downstairs. Really, that whistle! She opened the door of the sitting-room and looked around for the little girl she expected to see. She didn't notice the parrot, who was perched high up on the curtain-pole.

"Polly!" said Mrs Twiddle, looking all round. "Don't hide, dear. Where are you, Polly?"

"Bang-bang, you're dead!" said Polly from the curtain-pole, and gave a squeal of laughter. Poor Mrs Twiddle nearly jumped out of her skin. She stared up at the parrot, astounded. A parrot! How did that get here – and where was the little girl she expected?

"Milko! Milko! Two pints of bread and a loaf of milk!" said the parrot. "Bang-bang, you're…"

"Oh no, I can't bear it!" cried poor Mrs Twiddle, and ran into the garden.

"Twiddle, Twiddle, there's a parrot, a very rude parrot, in the sitting-room, and the little girl you fetched must have been frightened and has gone! Oh, Twiddle – what shall I do about the

parrot? Where did it come from?"

Twiddle stared at his wife in amazement. "But – but – you told me to fetch Polly from Miss Salt at Green Roofs!" he said. "And that's Polly. She's a parrot, not a girl."

"Twiddle! I told you to fetch Polly from Miss Pepper at Grey Roofs!" said Mrs Twiddle. "And you've brought a parrot home – a polly-parrot! Oh, whatever shall I do with you? And how can we get rid of the parrot? I'm scared of it!"

"So am I," said Twiddle. "Well..."

And just at that moment a little girl walked round the back way and into the garden – a dear little girl with golden hair and a big smile.

"Oh, excuse me," she said. "I couldn't make anyone hear, so I've come round the back. I waited and waited at Miss Pepper's to be fetched, but nobody came, so I've brought myself. Is that all right?"

"Oh, what a darling!" thought Mrs Twiddle and Mr Twiddle thought exactly the same thing. Soon they were both telling Polly about the silly mistake

Twiddle had made. How she laughed!

"I'll take Polly back to Miss Salt's for you," she said. "I know Polly very well – she's such a cheeky parrot."

And hey presto, she went indoors, grabbed the parrot, set her firmly on her shoulder and walked off. "I'll be back soon!" she called.

Mrs Twiddle turned and looked at Mr Twiddle. He waited for the huge scolding he was expecting. But instead Mrs

Twiddle was smiling.

"Isn't she sweet?" she said. "And didn't she laugh about your stupid mistake, Twiddle? Oh, I am going to enjoy having little Polly to stay, aren't you?"

"My word, yes!" said Twiddle, feeling suddenly happy again. "My word, yes! I'd rather have a hundred Polly-girls than one Polly-parrot! I'll go and meet her! I'll take her to have an ice cream! I'll buy her a doll, I'll…"

Now be careful, Twiddle – you'll have no money left soon!

When
the Sun Rises

It was night-time. Everywhere was dark. The little birds were all asleep in the trees and hedges and the rabbits were down in their holes. Only the red fox was out, hunting, and the big owl hooted as it looked for mice in the fields.

"The night is very long," said a little sparrow to his brother.

"It will soon be over now," said his brother.

"It is very cold," said a thrush, waking up and stretching his brown wings.

"When the sun rises it will be warm," said the blackbird.

A small rabbit put his head out of his burrow.

"I can see a grey light in the sky!" he called to his mother.

"Come here," said his mother. "The red fox is about. Wait till the sun rises and then you can go out safely, for the fox will go to his hole then."

The grey light in the sky grew brighter. Then slowly, slowly, it turned to pale gold – then to bright gold. The sun was coming!

"Chirrup-chirrup-chirrup!" twittered the sparrows, waking up one after another. "The sun is rising!"

The blackbird opened his orange beak and sang a song to welcome the sun. "The night was cold, so cold!" he sang. "But now the sky is gold!"

"Come and see, come and see, come and see!" sang the freckled thrush.

"Look, look!" cried the little rabbit, running out of his hole in the grass. "Here comes the big, round, golden sun!"

All the birds looked. Many rabbits came from their holes and watched. Some butterflies sleeping on the flowers awoke, stretched their pretty wings and fluttered up into the air to see the golden sun come slipping up into the sky. What

a big round ball it looked! How bright it was! How warm!

"The sky is red and gold!" called the starling from the tree-top. "The little clouds are red and gold too. I wish I had feathers of red and gold! How beautiful I should be!"

The rabbits scampered out into the early sunshine. They nibbled the grass. They were delighted to welcome the sun.

A lark awoke in the field. He felt the warmth of the rising sun on his brown feathers. He lifted up the crest on his head in delight. He had his nest in the field and his wife and babies were there. He was happy.

"Here is the beautiful sun again!" he sang to his wife. "I must fly up, up, up into the sky to get as near him as I can, and tell him all about our dear little family." So up he flew into the sky, up and up until the rabbits could only see a little black speck. But they could hear his beautiful song. It came pouring down from the sky as the lark flew higher and higher.

"I love the sun, the sun, the sun," he sang. "It warms my little ones, it makes the world so bright and lovely, I love the shining sun!"

"Pink, pink!" said the pretty little chaffinch, waking up in the hedge. "The clouds are pink, pink! The sun has risen again. It is daytime!"

The two robins flew to the hedgetop and sang their creamy song of joy. "Here is another lovely day. The sun went away last night and left the world dark and cold. Now he is back again and everything is beautiful! We love the sun!"

Peter's
New Shoes

Peter was proud of his new beach shoes. They were green, and on each toe there was a white piece of rubber in the shape of a little ship.

"Aren't they nice?" said Peter's mother. "Now listen, dear, I want you to wear these little shoes on the beach as well as when you paddle."

"Oh, why, Mummy?" said Peter. "I do like to feel the sand with my feet."

"I know you do," said his mother. "But yesterday I saw some broken glass on the beach, and I heard of a little girl who cut her foot on a piece. So I want you to keep your beach shoes on."

"People shouldn't leave broken glass about," said Peter. "It makes us wear shoes when we don't want to."

26

"It is very careless of people," said Mother. "But as I don't want you to get your feet cut, Peter, I'd like you to keep your shoes on, and to paddle in them too. Now don't forget."

Peter loved paddling. It was fun to go splish-splashing through the tiny waves. The stones didn't hurt his feet when he had his beach shoes on. Sometimes there was sand and sometimes there were stones. He didn't mind which if he had his shoes on.

Now that afternoon Peter was on the beach with Tinker the dog.

Peter thought he would build a big castle. He soon began, and Tinker got very excited and tried to dig too, sending the sand up into the air like a shower of spray.

"Hey! Stop, stop, Tinker!" said Peter. "That's not helping me! I don't like sand in my eyes."

The sand was warm in the sun. Peter's feet felt hot. He looked down at his new shoes.

"I wish I could take you off," he said. "You do make my feet hot."

"Woof!" said Tinker, and put his paw on Peter's foot.

"Yes, you needn't show me that you don't wear shoes," said Peter. "I know it already. I really think I'll take my shoes off for a little while. If I stay just here and don't go running over the beach I shall be all right."

So he took them off and set them neatly by his castle. Then he went on building it up, higher and higher and higher.

And do you know, by the time the

castle was finished, the sea was almost up to it. Peter was so excited! He shouted for joy. "I shall stand on top – I shall be king of the castle! Hurrah!"

He stood right on the top of his castle. He had made it very firmly indeed and patted it down well, so it was a very strong castle.

And then Peter suddenly remembered his beach shoes. "Oh dear! I must put them on again," he said. So he scrambled down to find them. But he must have put sand on top of them, because they couldn't be seen anywhere.

Mother came down to the beach, and shouted in surprise to see Peter's enormous castle. "What a big one!" she cried.

"Oh, Mummy, I've lost my shoes," said Peter in dismay, as he looked for them.

"But I told you not to take them off," said his mother, quite cross.

"Well, my feet were very hot, and I thought if I stayed here, just in one place, it wouldn't matter if I took them off for a little while," said Peter, going red.

"That was very naughty of you," said Mother. "I trusted you not to. Hurry up and find them and put them on."

But just then an enormous wave came and ran right round the castle – *splosh*! Peter only just jumped up in time or he would have been soaked through. His mother had to run ever so far back.

As soon as the wave had gone back, Peter got down from the castle and hunted about for his shoes once more but there wasn't any sign of them at all.

"The sea must have taken them," said the little boy sadly. "They're not here. Tinker, can't you find them?"

But Tinker couldn't, though he hunted too. Soon the sea was so far up the beach that Peter had to leave his castle and go and sit by the wall with his mother. She had his walking-shoes with her and he put them on.

"I suppose I can't paddle in these shoes," said Peter in a sad voice.

"Of course not," said Mother. "That's the worst of not doing as you are told – something horrible always happens! I am not going to punish you, because your shoes have punished you by getting lost, so that you can't paddle again."

Peter was very upset. It was such fun to paddle. He sat by his mother, looking very red. The sea made nice little waves and ran almost up to Peter. But he couldn't go and splash in them because he had lost his beach shoes.

Soon it was time to go home to tea. There was a little girl at the same house as Peter was staying at, and when she came in to tea her face was red with crying. Peter wondered why. But he didn't like to ask her. He thought perhaps she had lost her beach shoes too – but she hadn't, because he saw them by her spade.

"What are we going to do after tea, Mummy?" asked Peter.

"We'll go for a walk over the cliff and fly your kite," Mother said. "It's always so windy there."

"Oooh!" said Peter, pleased. It was fun to fly his kite up on the cliff. The wind pulled hard and the kite flew very high.

After tea he went to speak to Mandy,
the little girl. "Where's your new
bucket?" he said.

Tears came into Mandy's eyes. "Oh,
Peter," she said, "when I was playing
with it this afternoon a big wave came
and took it away. I couldn't get it back,
and now it's lost. And it was such a lovely
one."

"Oh, what a pity!" said Peter. "It was
the one with Mickey Mouse on, wasn't
it?"

"Yes," said Mandy. "I'm going to look
for it on the beach after tea. Mummy

says it may be left there when the tide goes down. Will you come and help me to look, Peter?"

"I can't," said Peter. "I'm going to the cliff to fly my kite."

"Oh, I do wish you weren't," said Mandy. "If only you'd help me I'm sure I could find my bucket. But the beach is too big to look all by myself."

Peter was a kind little boy. He badly wanted to fly his kite – but Mandy did need his help very badly too.

"Well, I'll come and help you instead of flying my kite," he said. "I lost my beach shoes this afternoon, so I know how horrid it is to lose something. I'll go and tell Mummy, and then we'll go to the beach together."

So in a little while Mandy and Peter were hunting all over the beach to see if the bucket had been left by the tide. The sea had gone down, and was leaving big stretches of seaweed, shells, and rubbish in crooked lines here and there. Peter and Mandy wandered up and down the long beach, looking hard.

It was dull work. Peter wished he was up on the cliff with his mother, flying his kite. He was sure he would not see Mandy's bucket. It would be just a waste of time.

But suddenly he did see it! It was under a pile of brown seaweed. He could see a bit of Mickey Mouse's red coat showing there quite clearly. He ran to it with a shout.

"I've got your bucket – I've got your
bucket!" he cried. He pulled it out of the
seaweed – and oh, whatever do you
suppose was inside the bucket? Guess!
Yes – one of Peter's green beach shoes!

"Oh! oh!" squealed Peter in delight.
"Here's one of my shoes in your bucket,
Mandy. Oh! Let's look for the other one.
It's sure to be near."

The two excited children looked hard – and soon Mandy gave a shout. "I've got it – I've got it! Look, it's under this little rock! It's full of shells! Oh, Peter, aren't we lucky! We've found all the things we lost."

They rushed home to their mothers. How pleased they were!

"Well, Peter, if you hadn't given up your kite-flying to help Mandy, I don't suppose either the bucket or your shoes would have been found," said Mother, hugging him. "So, though you were disobedient and lost your shoes, your kindness got them back. One was waiting for you in Mandy's bucket – that was funny!"

Peter always wears his shoes now, and never takes them off. So his feet are safe from glass and sharp tins. I hope yours are too!

Mr Twiddle
and the Soap

"Twiddle, those two children who are staying next door are really very tiresome," said Mrs Twiddle one day. "The poor cat is so scared of them that she sits indoors all day."

"Hm! That's a pity," said Twiddle. "I only feel kindly towards that cat when she's out of my sight. I thought I was falling over her more often than usual."

"Those children play at cowboys and Indians and yell in a most frightening manner," said Mrs Twiddle. "And yesterday, Twiddle, when I went out, something flew past my nose as I walked by the next door house."

"What do you mean? A bird or something?" said Twiddle, who wasn't really listening very hard.

"No. Of course I don't mean a bird," said Mrs Twiddle. "You're not listening, Twiddle. I'm sure it was something those children were shooting at me."

"Oh no – they wouldn't do that to a kind person like you," said Twiddle, quite shocked. "Why, children love you – they're always nice to you."

"Well I may be mistaken, but I still think that they shot something at me when I walked by," said Mrs Twiddle, poking the fire very hard indeed, and sounding quite cross. "I'm going out to

the shops in a minute and I shall be most annoyed if the same thing happens."

She put on her hat and marched out of the front door. Twiddle went to the window and watched. If those children shot something at his nice little wife he would certainly go and scold them!

But nothing seemed to happen. Mrs Twiddle walked along quite safely and didn't stop or jump as she would have done if something had hit her.

She came back half an hour later in a very bad temper. "When I walked by the

house next door as I was coming home just now, something shot past my nose again," she said. "It just touched the tip of it. I saw it. It's those children again."

"I'll go and walk by the house," said Twiddle, getting up. "Then if something is shot at me I'll go and give those two children such a telling-off. Ha! I know how to deal with children."

He marched out, hat on head, went through his front gate and turned to walk alongside the next door house. *Blip*! Something hit his hat, flew in the air and disappeared.

"What was that?" said Twiddle, startled. "I'll look for it – and when I find it I'll go and complain to the children's grandmother. Shooting at people like this! I never heard of such a thing in my life!"

He began to hunt about for whatever had hit him. A pea? An arrow? A dart of some kind? But however much he hunted he couldn't find any of these three things. Very strange! All he could see was a small piece of soap lying in the gutter, and he didn't take any notice of that, of course.

Whoosh! Something flew by his right ear and touched it smartly. Twiddle jumped. He glared at the windows of the house, but he couldn't see anyone. He was sure he could hear giggles, though.

"If I could just find what it was that hit my ear, I'd soon settle those children!" said Twiddle to himself. He looked down on the ground. Nothing lay there that could have hit him – but in the gutter he saw a second piece of soap. He stared at it.

"Dear me – who's been throwing soap away? Quite nice soap too. I've a good mind to pick it up and take it to Mrs Twiddle – she could mash it up together and use it for washing."

He bent down to pick up the soap, and something hit him smartly on the back and made him jump. He stood up crossly. Giggles again! Well, this time he certainly would go and complain to the children's grandmother.

He marched to the gate. Another bit of soap lay beside it. Twiddle picked it up –

three pieces for Mrs Twiddle now!

He walked up the path and knocked loudly on the door.

Nobody came. The door stayed shut. Twiddle knocked again. He knew there was somebody in the house – somebody who was quite good at shooting!

No answer. Twiddle walked round to the back and opened the kitchen door. Inside sat two children, and they looked most alarmed when they saw Twiddle walking in.

"Where's your grandmother?" said Twiddle, sternly. "I'm going to complain to her about you. You must be properly disciplined. Shooting people like this! Why, it's really dangerous!"

The boy and girl were twins and very alike. "Please," said the boy, "it isn't dangerous."

"But I tell you it is!" said Twiddle. "I don't know what sort of gun you use – or maybe it's a bow and arrows – but I must tell you that you nearly shot the tip off Mrs Twiddle's nose this morning, and almost got the top of my ear. Really shocking!"

"We don't use a gun or bows and arrows," said the girl, with a sudden giggle.

"Well, whatever it is I shall most certainly complain to your grandmother and as she is an old lady I shall offer to punish you myself, to save her the trouble," said Twiddle, quite fiercely. "And let me tell you this – I have a very hard hand, and also a very flappy slipper, which is just as good."

The girl screwed up her face and howled. Twiddle felt rather alarmed. Tears poured down the girl's face and the boy put his arm round her.

"You've made my sister cry," he said to Twiddle. "You're an unkind man. Go away."

Twiddle wasn't unkind. He began to feel very anxious. Dear me, was this girl never going to stop crying? There was quite a waterfall of tears down her dress!

"Don't cry," he said, and felt for his big handkerchief. "Here you are, wipe your eyes with this."

"What is it? A tablecloth?" said the boy, taking the enormous handkerchief. That made the girl laugh, and Twiddle was surprised to see somebody laughing and crying at the same time. The boy shook out the big hanky – and something fell out of it.

"Oh – you've got a bit of our soap," said the boy, picking it up.

"Your soap? What do you mean – your soap? I found bits of it lying all over the place outside," said Twiddle. "Do you go about dropping soap behind you?"

"No, we just squish it between our fingers and thumb," said the girl, wiping her eyes. "And it shoots off like a rocket!"

"Whatever do you mean?" said Twiddle, astonished. "Do wipe your eyes. I'm not a bit unkind really. I won't make you cry again."

"Well, you see," said the boy, "the other day Bella – that's my sister – and I were washing our hands in the cloakroom. I had a bit of soap in my hand – and I just gave it a bit of a squeeze – and it shot out

of my hand, out through the window –
and flew past Mr Grumpy's nose!"

"We didn't mean to," said Bella. "Did
we, Jim? It just popped out of his hand at
top speed. Soap is so slippery, you know.
Mr Grumpy got an awful shock."

47

"Serves him right," said Mr Twiddle, grinning suddenly. "Horrid, bad-tempered fellow." He stopped and frowned. "Er – no, I shouldn't have said that. Er – well forget that. So it was soap! What a dreadful waste to squish soap at everyone."

"It's only odd bits that our granny saves up to use for the washing," said Bella. "We go out and collect them again after we've squished them at people. We just couldn't help doing it, somehow."

"Very wrong of you," said Twiddle. "How exactly do you do the squishing?"

"Like this," said Jim. He took a piece of soap and wetted it at the tap. Then he squished it in his hand. It shot out at once, flew through the window and disappeared.

"Ha!" said, Twiddle, startled. "Well, well, what a thing to do! Don't you do it any more, that's all I can say. Er – let me have a squish."

Jim wetted another piece of soap and handed it to Mr Twiddle. He squeezed hard – a very good squish indeed – and it

48

hit a little vase of flowers and nearly overturned it.

"Oh, good shot!" said Jim and Bella together. Twiddle went rather red.

"Hm – I must go. I've wasted too much time with you already. Now, just remember – no more squishing bits of soap at people, see?"

"We promise," said the twins, beaming. Twiddle patted them both and gave them fifty pence each. He couldn't help liking them in spite of everything.

He went back to his house and Mrs Twiddle asked him at once what he had done.

"Did you go and scold those children? Are you going to tell their grandmother? I hope she will punish them well, little monkeys! I saw you going in looking very fierce indeed."

"Er – well, my dear, it's like this," began Twiddle, feeling rather embarrassed.

"Twiddle! Don't tell me you didn't scold them! Don't tell me you were as soft-hearted as usual and patted them on the head and gave them some money!" cried Mrs Twiddle.

"Now listen – I'll just show you how they shoot people," said Twiddle. "It all began as an accident. They're not going to do it again. Where's a bit of soap? Ah – here's one. I'll wet it. Now, you take it in your hand like this and you squeeze it hard – a really good squish – and off it flies, see?"

And off flew the bit of soap, straight out of the window, *whoosh*! Twiddle was

51

quite surprised to see how fast it went. So was Mrs Twiddle. She stared in horror.

The soap flew straight at somebody walking by their front hedge. *Whooosh*! It hit the person's flowery hat, and she gave a little scream. "Oh – what was that?"

"Twiddle! You've hit the children's grandmother – that bit of soap hit her hat!" whispered Mrs Twiddle. "Oh, how could you? Whatever will she say?"

The children's grandmother said quite a lot. She marched in and gave Twiddle such a scolding that he shook like a jelly – and what was more, Mrs Twiddle never said a word to help him!

"It serves you right," she said, when the angry old lady had gone. "Doing a thing like that! You're as bad as those children. No, you're worse! Learning their silly tricks! Behaving like an eight-year-old! Whatever you do—"

Twiddle began to feel desperate. He got up suddenly. "If you say a word more, do you know what I am going to do?" he said. "I'm going to get all the bits of soap in the house, sit at the kitchen window and squish them at your cat! Ha! If you think I'm so shocking, I will be shocking! I'll squish and I'll squish – and that will teach you what happens when you scold me without stopping!"

Well, of course kind Mr Twiddle would never have done such a thing, though he couldn't help thinking it would be a good way of keeping the cat out of the house. Mrs Twiddle caught his arm.

"No, don't , Twiddle! I won't scold you any more. Here's your paper, look, and there's a nice fire for you – and your slippers are ready to put on. Let's forget about the soap!"

Twiddle was pleased. He put on his

slippers, sat down by the fire and took up his paper. Now for a good long read!

Mrs Twiddle crept out of the room. She collected every bit of soap in the house and hid it. She wasn't going to trust Twiddle with bits of soap for quite a little while – you just never knew with Twiddle!

He'll be surprised when he next goes to wash his hands, won't he? No soap anywhere!

Mr Twiddle Cuts
the Grass

"I do wish," said Mrs Twiddle, "I do wish, Twiddle, that you would do something about that long grass in the garden. It looks so very untidy."

Mrs Twiddle said this almost every day. Mr Twiddle sighed. He knew he would have to cut that grass sooner or later. Well, it was a nice day. He might as well do it and get it over.

"Very well, my love," he said. "I'll take the scythe and cut it down. It's too long to mow. Anything to please you!"

"Well, put your garden trousers on, dear," said Mrs Twiddle. "You don't want to spoil your nice ones."

Mr Twiddle went upstairs and found his garden trousers. They were old grey flannel ones and he liked them. They were big and comfortable.

He put them on and then took everything out of the pockets of his other trousers and put them into the pockets of his garden trousers. In went his money, his keys, his handkerchief and a little roll of string that he always kept in case he might want some.

Then he went downstairs to find the scythe. "It may be blunt, of course," he said to Mrs Twiddle. "Then I couldn't start cutting the grass today."

"Well, it isn't blunt," said Mrs Twiddle. "I had it sharpened last week for you.

Now do get to work, Twiddle – you've been ages already getting your garden trousers on."

Twiddle went out into the garden. It was rather hot. Oh dear, scything was very, very hard work! He would soon be dreadfully hot! He took off his coat.

He walked to the long grass with the big scythe in his hand. Dear, dear, it certainly was very long! He felt the blade of the scythe to see if it really was sharp, and it was.

Now, just as Mr Twiddle was about to begin his work, the cat walked over to him and rubbed against his leg in a very loving manner. Twiddle was not very fond of his wife's cat. It always wanted doors or windows opened for it whenever Twiddle was sitting down reading his paper.

"Go away, Puss!" he said, sternly. "I'm going to do a bit of scything. You don't want your tail cut off, do you? Well, use your brains, then, and get away. Shoo!"

The cat rubbed itself against Mr Twiddle's other leg. Then it sat down

and began to roll in the grass.

"Did you hear what I said?" asked Twiddle. "Go away from this long grass. Right away. Surely you would not be silly enough to lie down and sleep in it just when I'm going to scythe it? Of course, I know that's just the kind of thing you would do!"

The cat immediately curled itself up in the grass and tucked its head into its paws. Twiddle stirred it with his foot.

"Now, what did I say? Go and find Mrs Twiddle! Go along!"

The cat uncurled itself, went a little way away, gave Twiddle a nasty look and settled down again. Mr Twiddle began to get angry. He ran at the cat.

"Shoo! Get away! Why do you always make things difficult for me?"

The cat decided that Twiddle wanted to have a game with it. It jumped up, crouched down, and ran at Twiddle's feet. Then it darted away into the grass and hid. Twiddle ran at it again. "Shoo! Will you go away and let me get on with my work?"

Mrs Twiddle put her head out of the window. "Twiddle! What are you doing rushing about in the grass all by yourself and shouting like that?"

"I'm not all by myself!" shouted back Twiddle, indignantly. "The cat's here. How can I cut the grass if she's darting about the whole time?"

He chased the cat all about the grass and at last it ran off to Mrs Twiddle, its tail straight up in the air. Twiddle, feeling very hot, panted a bit, and then lifted the scythe.

But just as he was about to begin he saw something lying in the grass, something bright and round. He picked it up. A ten-pence piece! Well, that was a nice little find. Very nice indeed. He put it into his pocket with his other money.

"It's a pity I can't find a bit more money," he said to himself. "If I could I'd pay a man to do this heavy scything."

He cut a piece of grass, and then he suddenly saw something shining once more. He bent down – goodness gracious, it was twenty pence!

"Very strange!" said Mr Twiddle. "Someone's been walking in this grass, I suppose, and dropped a bit of money. Who's been trespassing in my garden? Well, it serves him right to lose his money!"

He lifted his scythe again, and then thought that he might as well have a look to see if there was any more money lying in the long grass. So he put down his scythe and began to look.

He soon found five pence and two pence! Then he found another ten pence. Well, well, this was a nice surprise, to be sure! "Thirty-seven pence altogether. Splendid!"

He began to look very carefully indeed, bending down and peering in the grass, parting the long blades hopefully.

"Another twenty pence! Well, I never! And here's fifty pence. Would you believe it! Why, this bit of grass is full of money!"

It was most extraordinary. He kept on picking up five pences and two pences, ten pences and twenty pences, wherever he looked. He put them all into his pocket, feeling very pleased indeed. "I shall get a man to come and do the scything now. Why, I must have picked up about five pounds worth of money already. Very nice, very nice indeed!"

Mrs Twiddle looked out of the window again to see if Twiddle was getting on well with his scything. She saw him bending down, creeping here and there, then suddenly standing up to put something into his pocket, then bending down again and creeping about. What was he doing?

"Twiddle!" shouted Mrs Twiddle. "What do you think you're doing? Surely you're not playing with the cat?"

"I am not!" said Twiddle, standing up, looking rather hot. "I'm picking up money."

"Good gracious!" said Mrs Twiddle. "Money! Whatever do you mean?"

"What I say," said Twiddle, and bent down to pick up another ten-pence piece. He held it up to show her. "It's easy. I just look for it and I see it. It's all over this piece of grass. Wherever I go I find five pences and two pences and ten pences and twenty pences and fifty pences. Why, here's fifty pence by my foot now!"

So there was. Mrs Twiddle hurried down to the patch of long grass. "Really, Twiddle! I can't believe it. How could there be so much money in this grass? Where in the world did it come from?"

"Somebody must have dropped it," said Twiddle. "Somebody trespassing in my garden. Serves him right to lose it."

He picked up ten pence and put it into his pocket. "I'm going to pay a man to do this scything instead of me," he said. "And if you'd like to buy yourself a box of chocolates, I'd be pleased to give you the money. And we might perhaps buy a chicken for our dinner."

Mrs Twiddle looked very puzzled. She couldn't understand this money business at all. Twiddle wandered away a little and then picked up five pence. "See! I tell you wherever I go in this grass I pick up money."

"Your pocket must be absolutely full of it!" said Mrs Twiddle. "How much have you got?"

"Well, I've picked up dozens and dozens of five pences and ten pences and twenty pences and things," said Twiddle. "I'll show you what I've got."

He put his hand into his pocket to get out all the money he had put there. He felt round his pocket and a frown came on his face.

"What's the matter?" said Mrs Twiddle.

"A most extraordinary thing," said Twiddle, looking astonished, "I can't feel even a five-pence piece in my pocket! And yet I put dozens of coins there. Where have they all gone?"

"Let me feel," said Mrs Twiddle, and she put her hand into his pocket. She felt around and then she found a big hole at the bottom.

"Twiddle! You've got an enormous hole in that pocket. I really do think you are the stupidest man I've ever known! Here you go walking about with a hole in your pocket, dropping all your money out, and picking it up and putting it in your pocket again, then out it falls, and you

pick it up all over again – and think you're so rich we can have chicken for dinner!"

Mr Twiddle stared at his wife in dismay. He felt the hole in his pocket. "Have I – have I been picking up the same five pence and the same ten pence and the same twenty pence all the time?" he said. "Wasn't this grass full of money, then?"

"No, you stupid man! Whatever money

was here fell from your pocket – when you were chasing the cat about, I should think," said Mrs Twiddle. "And you kept on picking it up and losing it and picking it up – oh, Twiddle, I think my cat's got more sense in its head than you have. Wasting all the morning doing a silly thing like that!"

Twiddle was very upset. He picked up twenty pence by his foot and absent-mindedly put it into his pocket. It at once fell out and appeared by his foot again.

"See! That's what's been happening all the time," said Mrs Twiddle. "Now, you listen to me, Twiddle – I shan't give you any dinner at all till you've finished cutting this grass. So, if you want to play with the cat or go on picking up your money, you know what to expect!"

And little Mrs Twiddle walked back to the house quite crossly. Twiddle sighed loudly, took his scythe and set to work.

What a disappointment – and how cross Mrs Twiddle looked. Then a thought came into Mr Twiddle's head. He threw down his scythe and ran across

the garden till he came to the kitchen
window. He popped his head in and made
Mrs Twiddle jump.

"Now, you listen to me," said Twiddle,
quite fiercely. "Do you know whose fault
all this is? Yours, yours! And do you know
why? Because you didn't mend the hole
in my pocket! Aha! Aha!"

Then, feeling quite pleased with
himself, Twiddle went happily back to

the grass and scythed hard till it was all cut. And you will be glad to know that Mrs Twiddle had a lovely dinner ready for him, and gave him a hearty kiss when he came in.

"You're a dear old thing, even if you are stupid!" she said. "Now, don't you dare to say 'Aha!' to me again, or I shall laugh till I cry. Aha, indeed!"

The Boy
Next Door

Jeanie and Bob were pleased because at last someone had come to live in the house next door. It had been empty for a long time and it would be exciting to have someone living there again!

"I do hope there will be some children," said Jeanie. "It would be fun to have someone else to play with. It's a lovely garden next door, too – much nicer than ours. It would be fun to play in it."

Three days later when they looked out of their bedroom window, they saw a boy sitting in a deckchair in the garden, reading a book. He was about Bob's age, and the two children were pleased.

"Let's throw a ball over, and then when he gets it for us, we'll talk to him and see if he'll play with us," said Bob. So they threw a ball over, and waited for the boy to send it back. But he didn't. He saw the ball on the grass, but he just looked at it, and then turned back to his book again without getting it!

Jeanie and Bob looked through a hole in the fence and were cross. Lazy creature!

"May we have our ball, please?" called Jeanie.

"In a minute!" called the boy, and he went on reading his book. Jeanie and Bob were very angry. Presently the boy's mother came out to speak to him and the boy said something and pointed to the ball. His mother picked it up and threw it back. Bob was most disgusted.

"Lazy, stuck-up creature!" he grumbled to Jeanie. "Fancy waiting till his mother came out and then making her get it for us! He must be a selfish, spoilt boy. We won't have anything to do with him."

The next day Jeanie had a fine blue balloon which she blew up very big indeed. The wind pulled the string out of her hand and the balloon flew over into the next garden! Jeanie stared in dismay. She peeped over the fence and saw the boy there, reading again. He had seen the blue balloon but he hadn't got up to get it! No, he was just watching it drift across the garden. Jeanie saw that it was blowing near a prickly holly-bush and she was afraid it would burst on a thorn.

"Oh quick, quick, get my balloon for me!" she cried. "It will burst!"

Just at that moment there was a loud pop and the balloon, which had drifted against the holly, burst into rags. Jeanie

was angry and unhappy. She slipped down from the fence, saying loudly, "You horrid, unkind boy!" She ran to tell Bob, and the two children said all sorts of rude, unkind things very loudly indeed by the fence. There was no answer from the boy, so they hoped he was feeling ashamed of himself. Their mother heard them saying these unkind things, and she was shocked.

"No matter how selfish or unkind you think others are you have no right to be rude and unkind yourself to them," she said. "That is making yourself as bad as they are."

When the children went to school the next day someone told them that the boy next door was going to their school the following week.

"Oh!" said Bob, turning up his nose. "Well, I shan't speak to him then! He's a mean, selfish, stuck-up creature, and Jeanie and I won't have anything to do with him!"

"Why?" asked the other children, surprised. So Bob and Jeanie told them about their ball and balloon, and the other children were most disgusted. "We won't be friends with him, either!" they said.

So when the boy, whose name was John, came to their school the next week, all smiles and most eager to be friends, no one would have anything to do with him.

John was puzzled. He usually got on very well indeed with other boys and girls. Why was everyone so horrid to him here? Jeanie and Bob especially were quite rude. John worried very much and his mother asked him what the matter

was, for she didn't like to see him frowning when he came home from school.

John wouldn't tell her why, for he thought she would be sure to worry about him if he didn't like his new school. "I must find out what's the matter with the children myself," he thought. So the next day he asked a little girl called Mary why no one would be friends with him.

"Well, we heard you were a horrid, unkind, stuck-up boy," said Mary. "That's why we don't like you."

John was more puzzled than ever. "But no one knows anything about me!" he said. "I've only just come to this school."

"Oh, Jeanie and Bob know a lot about you, because they live next door to you," said Mary. "They told us about you."

John felt angry. Why should Jeanie and Bob say such horrid things about him? Why, he had hardly spoken to them! He went up to Jeanie and Bob, frowning.

"Look here!" he said. "I've just heard that you've been telling everyone I'm horrid and unkind. It isn't fair of you.

You don't know anything about me!"

"Oh yes we do!" said Jeanie, at once. "You wouldn't throw us back our ball when it went into your garden. You made your mother throw it back instead. And when my balloon flew over, you let it burst rather than get up and catch it for me."

"So of course we think you're lazy, stuck-up, selfish, unkind and everything else!" said Bob. "And you must be, too, to do things like that!"

John listened and went very red.

"Now I'm going to tell you something," he said. "I may have seemed all those things to you but I had sprained my ankle last week and the doctor wouldn't let me walk on it at all. Mum made me promise not to get up from my chair in the garden, though I longed to often enough. I saw your ball and your balloon, but I couldn't get them for you, though I wanted to – and I was awfully sorry when the balloon burst. I kept calling out to you that I was sorry, but you were shouting something yourselves, I don't know what, so I suppose you didn't hear me."

John walked away. Jeanie and Bob looked at one another. Both their faces were as red as beetroots. They felt dreadfully ashamed of themselves. So that was why the boy next door hadn't got their ball for them or saved their balloon from bursting. He hadn't been able to use his bad foot!

"Jeanie, it was horrid of us to think and say all we did," said Bob, in a low voice. "We've told stories about him, you know, though we thought they were true. We behaved much worse than we

thought John did. We might have given him a chance. What shall we do?"

Jeanie's eyes were full of tears. She was very sorry for what she had said and done. John had seemed so nice when he had spoken to them just now – he hadn't scolded them or called them names. He had just explained why he had seemed so horrid the week before.

"I'm going to tell everyone what a mistake we made," said Jeanie, wiping her eyes. "Then I'm going to say I'm sorry to John. He won't want to speak to us again, I'm sure, or play with us, but I must say I'm sorry."

"I will too," said Bob. John was gone by then, but some of the other children were about. Jeanie and Bob went up to them and told them everything.

"Well! Fancy that!" they said. "So he's quite a nice boy after all! It was wrong of you, Jeanie and Bob, to act like that. You're not so nice as we thought you were."

Jeanie and Bob went home, sad and upset. In the garden next door the boy was playing with a splendid bicycle. Jeanie saw him. "Come along," she said to Bob. "We'll tell him we're sorry, now, we've got a good chance." So they went to the fence and called John. He came at once.

"John," said Bob, through the hole in the fence. "We know you won't want to speak to us or play with us at all after what we've done, but Jeanie and I just wanted to tell you that we're very sorry indeed. It was horrid of us to behave like that. We've told the other children that we were quite wrong about you. Please forgive us. Goodbye!"

"Wait a minute! Don't go away!" said the boy next door. He hoisted himself up

to the top of the fence. "Don't worry about things! It's good of you to say you're sorry and tell all the other children the truth. Let's forget about it, shall we? I do so want to play with you. Come over and have a ride on my new bike. My mother gave it to me for being good about my bad ankle and not walking on it till it was quite better!"

Wasn't that nice of John? In no time at all the children were all playing happily together in John's garden – and if you ask Jeanie or Bob now who their best friend is, they will both answer together: "The boy next door, of course!"

Mr Twiddle
Gets a Fright

"I shall be late home tonight, my dear," said Mr Twiddle, putting on a macintosh. "Good gracious, this coat is tight – I must be getting fat."

"No wonder it feels tight – it's my mac you are putting on, Twiddle," said Mrs Twiddle, vexed. "There, now you've torn the armhole. I never knew such a man."

Twiddle went to get his own mac, glad he wasn't getting fat after all.

"What's all this about you being late home tonight?" said Mrs Twiddle. "I thought you were just going to Mr Jolly's to borrow a book."

"Yes, I was," said Twiddle. "But he is speaking at a meeting and asked me to go and hear him. So I said I would. But he's going in his car so he will bring me right back to the door. You needn't worry about me."

"I'll have some hot cocoa ready for you," said Mrs Twiddle. "And I'll spend a nice quiet evening mending the armhole of my mac!"

Twiddle went off to Mr Jolly's. He forgot to take his umbrella, so he was very wet when he got to his friend's house. Mrs Jolly took his mac to dry it, and Mr Jolly took him indoors to a nice big fire. "It's good of you to come to my meeting tonight," he said. "I can do with an extra person to clap me!"

"Oh, I'll clap you all right," said Twiddle, who liked plump Mr Jolly very much. "Now, if you'd just look out a book to lend me…"

"Right," said Mr Jolly. "What sort? A nice quiet story?"

"No, no, I think I'll have a really exciting one," said Twiddle. "You know – about stolen cars, and kidnapping and disappearances – things like that."

"Dear me – I wouldn't have thought you were the kind of person to want a book like that," said Mr Jolly, surprised.

"Well, my life is very quiet," said Twiddle, "and as I shall never be mixed up in robberies or kidnappings and things like that, it's fun to read about them. Mrs Twiddle never will get me an exciting book from the library – she says it makes me talk in my sleep. But I'm sure I don't!"

Mr Jolly and Mr Twiddle spent a pleasant half-hour looking for a really exciting book, then it was time to go to the meeting. "I'll just get out my car," said Mr Jolly. "It's very dark tonight –

and a bit foggy too – what a nuisance!"

Soon Twiddle heard Mr Jolly hooting outside the front door, and he hurried out with Mrs Jolly, who was going too. He got into the little car and sat at the back, feeling very comfortable. Off they went.

The meeting was very dull. Even Mr Jolly couldn't keep Twiddle awake! Mrs Jolly, who was sitting next to him, had to keep nudging him, because she was afraid that he would begin snoring. Twiddle was glad when the meeting was over. He had unfortunately had a nap while Mr Jolly was making his speech, which was a pity. Mr Jolly had seen him asleep and was not pleased with him!

"I just have to speak to a few people before I drive off," he said to Mr Twiddle. "You go and sit in the back of the car, and Mrs Jolly and I will join you in a few minutes."

"Right," said Twiddle and he went out into the dark, foggy night. He opened the door of the car and got in at the back. Brrrrrr! It was cold! He fumbled in the front of the car and found a rug. He wrapped it right round him, and felt nice and cosy at once. You can guess what he did next – he fell asleep!

He woke up when the car started. At first he couldn't remember where he was and he was scared.

"Of course, I came out of the meeting and got into Mr Jolly's car – and I must have fallen asleep," thought Twiddle. "Dear me, I'd better congratulate Mr Jolly on his speech – though I can't seem to remember a word of it!"

He bent forward to say a few kind words to the driver. Just then the car passed under a streetlamp, and Twiddle got a terrible fright. The driver was not Mr Jolly! Most decidedly he was not the round, fat-faced Mr Jolly! This driver was thin and he wore a checked cap, which Mr Jolly never did. Who was this man at the wheel of Mr Jolly's car, then?

Twiddle shrank back into his corner. It must be a car-thief! Someone who had stepped into Mr Jolly's car, never dreaming there was anyone sitting at the back – and now he was driving away into the night, goodness knows where!

Twiddle was frightened. What would this car-thief say when he discovered

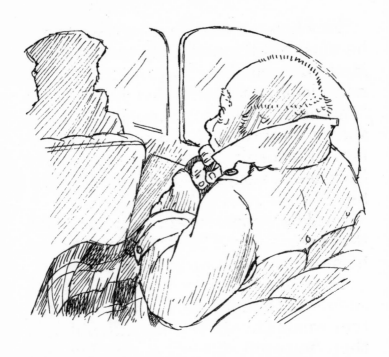

him? Would he hit him – or throw him out into the road? Twiddle's heart began to beat fast.

He thought of Mr Jolly. Whatever would he say when he found out that his car had been stolen? Would he guess that Twiddle had been stolen with it? What would Mrs Twiddle say when he didn't come home? Twiddle was so upset that he almost groaned.

Somehow he must escape. Somehow he must tell the police about this thief. He took a good look at him. "What a nasty looking fellow!" thought Twiddle. "Big nose, moustache much too long, shaggy eyebrows, I can just see them now he's turning to look at something. Goodness, I wouldn't like to have to fight him."

Twiddle wondered where in the world they were going. They sped on and on – he must be a long way from home!

They came to a town. Twiddle suddenly thought of an idea. Perhaps they would have to stop at traffic lights – then he could slip out of the car and report this man as a thief. Yes – that was a really fine idea!

They came, at last, to traffic lights. Twiddle hoped and hoped they would turn to red – yes, just as they came up to them the amber light showed, and then the red. The car stopped. Twiddle began to fumble with the door handle but it was stiff and he couldn't move it. The noise he made caused the driver to turn round. When he saw Twiddle in the car he was amazed. "Here, you! What are you doing here?" he yelled.

"What are *you* doing here?" yelled back Twiddle, sounding much braver than he felt. "You thief!"

"Now then – what do you mean by that?" said the man. "How dare you slink into the back of my car? I'll drive you straight to the police station!"

"Yes, do!" said Twiddle. "I'll report you there – that'll suit me fine. I was just trying to get out of this car to find a policeman."

"Do you expect me to believe that?" said the man. "You were hoping to slip out without my seeing you!"

The sudden noise of the cars behind, hooting loudly, made both the driver and Mr Twiddle jump. The traffic lights had turned green and they hadn't noticed – but the cars behind wanted to get on and they were hooting madly. The driver of the car Twiddle was in started off with a sudden jerk and Twiddle almost fell off the seat.

He sat back in despair. He had lost his chance. He hadn't been able to slip out of the car. Now the driver would go on and on and on, and when he came to a lonely place, he would attack poor Twiddle and dump him somewhere! Twiddle didn't feel at all happy.

But in one minute the driver stopped again. Twiddle peered out to see where they were – and, oh joy, they had stopped outside a police station! Had the police stopped them? Perhaps they had noticed the stolen car and had stopped it to arrest the driver. Just then the driver hooted

loudly, and a policeman came running out of the police station. The driver slid down his window and spoke loudly to him.

"There's a man at the back of my car who has no right to be there. He slipped into it when my car was parked. I'd like you to arrest him."

Twiddle was simply amazed. Arrest him! Why, he was going to tell the police to arrest the driver! What cheek he had to tell them to arrest him, Twiddle!

Twiddle was pulled out of the car and taken into the police station. The driver followed, looking very tall and fierce. Twiddle pointed at him. "Arrest that man!" he said. "He has stolen my friend's car."

"Nonsense – the fellow's mad!" said the other man, his moustache bristling fiercely. "See – here is my motor insurance!"

He handed it to the policeman, who at once sent a man to check it with the number of the car. Twiddle glared at the other man. "You're a thief! There was I,

sitting in my friend's car, having a snooze – and you drove off with it. I'd just come out of a meeting and—"

"Oh – so you went to the meeting, too, did you?" said the other man. "I don't believe you. Who's your friend, anyway?"

"Mr Jolly – he spoke at the meeting," said Twiddle, just as fiercely.

"Yes, he did – and just you tell me what he said," said the other man. "Go on – if you can tell me what his speech was about, I'll believe you."

Poor Twiddle! He had slept all through Mr Jolly's speech and he couldn't remember a word of it. He went very red and said nothing.

"There!" said the other man, "all a lot of fairytales! He didn't go to the meeting, he never heard a word of the speeches, he doesn't even know Mr Jolly. Well, I do – he's my cousin."

"Ooooh, you fibber!" said Twiddle. "You know you're a car-thief."

"Now, now, steady on," said the policeman. "He's Sir Dumbleby-Dickson – his motor insurance says so – and it is

the insurance for that car outside. You've made a mistake, you know!"

Twiddle gaped. What! That car did belong to this man? It wasn't Mr Jolly's? But then – how – how ... what had happened then?

And then, of course, poor Twiddle suddenly knew what he had done. He had got into the wrong car! He hadn't slipped into Mr Jolly's car – he had got into Sir Dumbleby-Dickson's. He had called him a car-thief! He had said simply terrible things to him!

"I've made a mistake," mumbled Twiddle. "I'm sorry. I apologise. I apologise most humbly. I got into the wrong car. It couldn't have been Mr Jolly's."

"Are you really a friend of Mr Jolly's?" said Sir Dumbleby-Dickson. "What's your name?"

"Twiddle," said Mr Twiddle. "Jolly's known me for years."

"Twiddle!" said Sir Dumbleby-Dickson, and held out his hand. "Dear me, my cousin Jolly has often spoken of you. The tales he's told me of you – I've laughed and laughed! Honestly, I couldn't believe that anyone could do the extraordinary

things you do, Mr Twiddle, or make such peculiar mistakes – I couldn't! But I see he's right. Ha-ha-ha, what a joke to tell my friends! You're *exactly* like Jolly said!"

Twiddle didn't really feel pleased to hear all this, though he was glad that Sir Dumbleby-Dickson believed him. He shook hands solemnly, and didn't say a word.

"Well, I must be off," said Sir Dumbleby-Dickson. "I'm late as it is. So glad to have met the famous Mr Twiddle at last, and to have such a joke about him to tell everyone. Ho-ho-ho – I shall laugh every time I think of you!"

Off he went, and Twiddle heard his car roaring away into the night. Now poor Twiddle has got to get home somehow – and I have a feeling he will be very late back, and that he will find it very, very difficult to explain everything to Mrs Twiddle.

"Why do I do things like this?" groaned Twiddle.

I don't know, Twiddle – but I'm quite glad you do!

Mr Twiddle
Pays a Call

"Twiddle dear," said Mrs Twiddle, "you know a lot about trees. What's that one called that has pretty little round balls hanging on it?"

"A plane tree?" said Twiddle.

"No, dear, it's not at all a plain tree," said Mrs Twiddle. "It's quite a pretty one."

"I said plane, not plain," said Twiddle. "Not p-l-a-i-n, but p-l-a-n-e."

"Oh. Well, why don't you say what you mean, Twiddle," said Mrs Twiddle. "It's in Mrs Brown's garden. As you pass by today, just pop in and tell her you've come to look at the tree – and see if you can give her its name. It's such a pretty one."

"Right," said Twiddle, and off he went

for his walk. Halfway down the next road he suddenly wondered which house was Mrs Brown's. Was it number 8 or number 18? He asked a milkman.

"Mrs Brown's – oh that's round the corner – house called Whitewalls," said the milkman. "Mind the dog there – it can be nasty."

"Oh – thank you," said Twiddle, and he went on round the corner. He saw Whitewalls and crossed over to it. There was a rather fierce-looking dog sitting on the front doorstep, and it growled deeply at Twiddle.

"Well, if you won't let me ring the bell or knock, I shall go to the back door, you ill-mannered dog," said Twiddle. And away he went round the side. He knocked at the back door and a cross-looking woman came to open it.

"Er – good morning, Mrs Brown – I've come to have a look at your—" began Mr Twiddle, but the woman didn't let him finish.

"I've been expecting you for a whole hour," she said. "You've prevented my going out to do my shopping! Come along in, and give me your advice. Oh – there's the dog come in at the back door, just when I'd shut him out at the front!"

"Gr-r-r-r," said the dog, eyeing Mr Twiddle's ankles.

"Be careful of him. He doesn't like strangers," said Mrs Brown, and led the way into a sitting-room.

"But surely the tree is in the garden?" said Twiddle, puzzled, and skipped quickly out of the way as the dog sniffed round his feet.

"Now, look – it's this window," said

Mrs Brown. "I want your advice. It simply will not shut, and I'm so afraid of burglars, you know!"

The dog barked loudly at the word burglars, and made Twiddle jump.

"I shouldn't have thought you needed to be afraid of burglars with *this* dog about," he said. He stared at the window, watching Mrs Brown trying to shut it.

"You'll break it if you bang it like that," said Twiddle. "You'll never shut it that way."

"Well, how shall I shut it?" said Mrs Brown, crossly. "You've come to give me advice, haven't you?"

"Yes, but only about—" began Twiddle, and jumped up on a chair as the dog nipped his trouser-leg. "I say – do shut your dog out of the front door again. And honestly, all you want is a spot of oil on the hinges of that window."

"Well, why didn't you say so?" said Mrs Brown and disappeared into the next room, where Twiddle heard her rummaging about. He felt inclined to slip out of the house and go home. He had only come to name a tree – and here he was, being expected to mend a window, with a very bad-tempered dog watching his every movement.

"You'd love to nip me if I gave you a chance, wouldn't you?" he said to the dog. "I don't like you. I wouldn't have you for a pet at any price!"

"Gr-r-r-r-!" said the dog, rudely.

Mrs Brown came back with a big oil-can. She pushed it at Twiddle. "Here you are. I've just filled it, so there's plenty of oil. See what you can do with the hinges – if it *is* the hinges that are causing the trouble, which I very much doubt."

Twiddle thought that Mrs Brown was almost as rude as her dog! He took the oil-can, which immediately dripped oil all down his trousers. Goodness – now what would Mrs Twiddle say! His trousers had only just come back from the cleaners.

"Look at that – on my clean trousers!" he said in dismay.

"Well, why don't you wear dirty ones?" said Mrs Brown, and Twiddle felt so cross that he wished he could tip the oil-can down her neck. How *could* nice little Mrs

Twiddle be friends with this horrid Mrs Brown?

He began to drip a little oil on to the hinges of the window. "It's running down on to the windowsill," said Mrs Brown. "Look!"

"Well, have you got a rag or a cloth to wipe it with?" said Twiddle. "You can't help oil dripping down!"

"I should have thought you would have brought your own rag," said Mrs Brown. "Good gracious me, I don't know what you men are coming to!"

Twiddle turned round indignantly, and the oil-can swung above the dog's head. Two drops of oil fell on it and the dog yelped and put its paw up to scrape it off.

"Oh – sorry," said Twiddle, hastily swinging the oil-can to the window again. "Never mind – a drop of oil won't hurt him."

"But look what he's doing!" cried Mrs Brown. "Rubbing his head on my clean couch! Really, you are careless!"

Twiddle began to feel very cross

indeed. He pursed up his lips and frowned while he oiled the hinges carefully. Then he set down the can and began to move the window to and fro, to let the oil penetrate properly.

"No creaking now," he said, and shut the window. "There! It shuts!"

"Thank goodness," said Mrs Brown. "Now I'd like you to look at my bathroom tap, if you will. It keeps on running and running."

Twiddle didn't see why he should do any more jobs for this unpleasant woman. He began to wonder if his wife knew she had wanted little jobs done and sent Twiddle along to do them, pretending she wanted him to name a tree. If Mrs Twiddle had done that, Twiddle was going to say some very cross things to her when he got home.

"I don't think I've got time to stay any longer," he said, looking at his watch. "I really only just popped in to see that tree, you know, and I—"

"Now come along, I want you to see the tap, as well as the window," said Mrs Brown, firmly, and went upstairs. Twiddle had to go too because the dog bumped its nose against the back of his legs, making him scuttle upstairs quickly behind Mrs Brown. He looked at the dribbling tap in the bathroom and nodded. "It needs a washer," he said.

"Did you bring one?" asked Mrs Brown.

"Of course not. Why should I?" said Twiddle, surprised. "I didn't know I was going to see a dripping tap. I thought I was going to see a tree."

"A tree! There's nothing wrong with any tree as far as I know," said Mrs Brown, opening a cupboard to see if she had a spare washer somewhere.

"Well, it wasn't something wrong with it, it was just to – ooh, here's that dog again," said Twiddle. "I do wish you

wouldn't let it growl at me like that. I know it will fly at me in a minute."

"Well, I'll get it away from you if it does," said Mrs Brown, impatiently. "See, here's the washer. You'll have to turn off the water at the main before you take off the tap."

"I know, I know," said Twiddle, beginning to feel snappy. "Well, if your dog will allow me to squeeze out of the door I'll go and find the mains tap."

The dog allowed him to go downstairs, but followed him closely all the time. Twiddle managed to find the mains tap and turn it off, and then went back to the bathroom. He put on the new washer quite quickly.

"Thanks," said the woman, as they went downstairs again. "I think that's about all."

"Well – what about this tree in your garden," said Twiddle. "Shall I see if I know its name?"

"Tree? Whatever do you mean? You and your trees!" said Mrs Brown. "Look out of that back window there – there's

only one tree in my garden and anybody knows what that is. It's full of roses, so it's a rose-tree!"

Twiddle stared out into the back garden. Sure enough, there was only one tree there – a rose-tree. He was astonished.

"How much do I owe you for those two jobs?" asked Mrs Brown, getting out her purse.

"Mrs Brown – who do you think I am?" asked Twiddle, startled. "I don't charge for doing little services to my friends."

"But aren't you the odd-job man from the builders up the road?" said Mrs Brown, in astonishment.

"No," said Twiddle, also astonished. "I'm Mr Twiddle, and my wife is a friend of yours."

"But I don't know any Mrs Twiddle," said Mrs Brown. "You've come to the wrong house! There's a Mrs Brown in the next road – that's the one you want, if you're longing to name trees. She's got quite a forest for a garden!"

Twiddle decided he wouldn't stop for another minute. He hurried out, and shut the front gate firmly on the dog. The wrong Mrs Brown? And he had spent all the morning doing silly jobs for somebody he didn't know at all!

He came to house Number 18 in the next road, and saw that there were dozens and dozens of different trees in the garden there. But Twiddle wasn't going to visit any more Mrs Browns that morning. He was going home for a cup of coffee!

"And I shan't tell Mrs Twiddle a single

thing about what I've done this morning!" he thought. "She'd laugh till she cried!"

But Twiddle – what are you going to say when Mrs Twiddle asks you how you made your trousers so oily? You *are* going to find things difficult!

The Busy
Little Postmen

A bee stood on a stalk and cleaned his front legs carefully. A small lizard looked up and saw him.

"Bee!" he said. "Come down and talk!"

"Too busy," said the bee.

"Busy! You're not! Why, you do nothing but suck honey!" cried the lizard. "I'll come up the stalk and snap at you if you tell stories like that!"

"Well, I shall sting you if you do," said the bee. "I'm telling you the truth. I'm too busy to play with you. My friends and I are the flowers' postmen. We are kept very busy delivering for the flowers all day long."

"What do you deliver?" said the lizard in wonder. "Letters?"

"No, you silly lizard! We deliver the

pollen from one flower to another!" said the bee, importantly. "Didn't you know that? Flowers can make seeds by themselves, it is true, but didn't you know that most of them employ us as postmen, and get us to deliver the pollen to their neighbours for them?"

"Well, I never knew that before," said the lizard. "How do you carry the pollen from one flower to another, bee? Have you a bag or a box or something?"

"No. The flower spills its pollen on my back or my head, or wherever it likes," said the bee. "Come and watch, if you like. Look, I'm going into this flower, quite cleaned up – watch what I'm like when I come out!"

He squeezed himself into a flower. When he came out he was dusted with golden pollen all down his back! The lizard laughed.

"You look like a very dusty bee now," he said. "Go into another flower and let me see what happens then."

The bee squeezed into another flower. The lizard peeped in to see what happened. He saw that the pollen was rubbed off against the seed-box of the flower, and that some of the tiny grains were left there.

"Did you see that?" asked the bee, coming out backwards on to the lizard's nose. "I've delivered some pollen there. Now that flower can begin to make seed. It's a clever idea, isn't it?"

"Oh yes!" said the lizard. "Very clever! I didn't know that before. But bee – how

very, very, very kind of you to work so hard for the flowers! I suppose you don't get any wages at all?"

"Of course I do," said the bee. "You don't suppose I'd work for nothing, do you? No, the flowers pay me and all the other bees very well indeed. They make honey for us, and we take it in return for our postman work. And very delicious honey it is too – pure nectar!"

"Give me a taste!" begged the lizard. But the bee wouldn't.

"Too buzzzzzzzzzy!" he buzzed, and flew off. Clever little postman, isn't he?

Mr Twiddle's Cold

"Don't you feel well, Twiddle?" asked Mrs Twiddle one morning. "You didn't want your breakfast, and you keep sniffing."

"Well – perhaps I don't feel very well," said Twiddle, frowning. "My throat's a bit sore. I'd better not go out and chop all the wood, had I?"

"Well, I don't know about that," said Mrs Twiddle. "It's a nice sunny day and it might do you good to get out and chop the wood. You might have an appetite for your lunch then."

Twiddle immediately felt sure that his throat was very bad, and he gave a little cough. "I believe I'm going to have a cough, too," he said. "I really do not feel well. I can't chop wood this morning."

"Well, you can turn out all the drawers in that big cupboard over there, then," said Mrs Twiddle. "You've been saying for months that you never have time to – now you've got all the morning, if you don't go out and chop the wood."

"I don't think I feel well enough to turn out drawers either," said Twiddle, and gave another loud sniff. "Dear me – where's my hanky? I'm afraid I've got a heavy cold coming on. I'd better go and keep warm by the fire, my love."

He gave such a deep, hollow cough that Mrs Twiddle was quite startled. She looked at him. Now – was he pretending, or was he not? He did look a little pale. Perhaps he *was* sickening for something.

"I'll just call in at the doctor's when I'm out and ask him to come along and see you," she said. "Now, if he comes, please be polite, and offer him a cup of tea and a piece of my cake on this cold day."

"The doctor's away," said Twiddle, settling himself into his chair. "Oh, get off my knee, cat! Why does this cat always jump on my knee when I sit down?"

"Let the cat be," said Mrs Twiddle. "It's lazy like you, and likes a warm sit-down when it can get it. I know the doctor's away, but there's another one come to take his place till he comes back. And very, very clever he is, too, so I've heard tell. Very up-to-date, with plenty of new ideas and new ways. Now, don't you fall fast asleep, Twiddle – you keep awake and let him in when he knocks."

"All right, all right," said Twiddle, opening his newspaper. "Bless me, here's

that cat again. Can't you take her out with you, dear?"

"Don't be silly, Twiddle," said Mrs Twiddle, bustling about. "Now, I'll leave the kettle on for you to make tea when the doctor comes – and the biscuits on a plate – and the cake's there in its tin. Now, don't forget."

"Anyone would think I was giving a tea-party," grumbled Twiddle, and began to read the paper. Soon he heard Mrs Twiddle calling goodbye, and then the front door slammed. Good. Now he would have a bit of peace! He shut his eyes and in half a minute he was sleeping soundly. The cat got back on his knee and purred contentedly.

At about eleven o'clock there came a knock at the front door – *rat-tat-tat*! Twiddle woke up and the cat leaped off his knee in fright. *Rat-tat-tat*! The knocking came again.

"It's the doctor," said Twiddle, and got up in a hurry. "Now, I mustn't forget to offer him something to eat and drink."

He went to the front door and opened

it, wondering what sort of fellow the new doctor was. A very tall man stood there, with a thick beard, carrying a small black bag in his hand.

"Come in, come in," said Twiddle. "I'm sorry to call you out on a day like this – so cold and miserable. But I've got the kettle on for a cup of tea! Come along in."

The man looked pleased. He followed Twiddle in and watched him turn up the gas under the kettle in the kitchen. Then he looked at the biscuits with pleasure.

"Sit down," said Twiddle. "I won't be

long making the tea. You do like tea, don't you?"

"Well, it'll be nice to have a warm drink," said his visitor, and went to sit down by the fire. Twiddle made some tea and then brought in the big pot. He cut some of Mrs Twiddle's cherry cake and put that on a plate too.

The visitor ate a large slice and took some biscuits too. "A very good cake," he said. "Well now – I suppose we'd better get to work. Would you stand up please?"

Twiddle stood up. The man undid his bag and Twiddle looked inside. There were scissors of all sizes there, and a knife, besides several other things.

"Would you stretch out your arms, Mr Twiddle?" said the man, and took a tape measure from his bag. "First the right – thank you. Now the left. Thank you."

"Aha – new ways and methods!" said Twiddle, jokingly. "Measuring instead of medicine, I suppose? I quite thought you'd want to see my throat!"

"Well – I'll have to measure that too,"

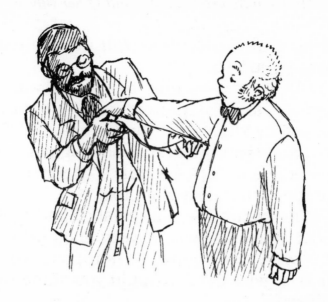

said the man, looking rather puzzled. "And now will you please bend your elbow, sir? I must just run my measure from shoulder to elbow and elbow to wrist."

Mr Twiddle began to fumble for his handkerchief, for he felt a sneeze coming. It came – and it was a most enormous one: "*A-whoooosh-ooo!*"

"Sorry," said Twiddle. "I really have got a nasty cold."

"So your wife told me when she asked me to call this morning," said his visitor, writing something down in a notebook. "I was sorry to hear it."

"Don't you take the temperatures of the people you call on?" asked Twiddle, who loved his being taken.

The man looked at him in surprise, decided it was a joke, and laughed loudly.

"Ha, ha! Not usually, sir. It would be rather a waste of time, wouldn't it?"

Twiddle began to feel that there was something rather peculiar about this doctor. Why should taking a temperature be a waste of time? Usually it was the first thing a doctor did when he came to see a patient.

"Well, I should have thought it was a waste of time measuring my arms," he said. "But still I suppose it's something new and up-to-date."

"Er – well – no, not exactly," said the man, who was now beginning to look a little alarmed himself. He did a little more measuring, and Twiddle began to feel tired of it. He sat down in the chair.

"Don't you think I ought to go to bed?" he asked. "And aren't you going to look at

my tongue?" He stuck it out and the
man backed away at once.

"Er – well – it looks quite a good
tongue," he said. "Quite. But I don't
usually look at tongues – unless you want
me to measure yours, do you? Ha, ha,
ha!"

Twiddle began to feel that he didn't
like this doctor at all. He might be very
modern and up-to-date with a lot of new
ways – but he was silly, really silly. Didn't
he know that doctors always looked at
tongues? He asked another question.

"Er – I suppose it wouldn't be at all good for me to go out and chop wood this morning, would it?" he asked, hoping that the man would say no, certainly he must not go out and chop wood.

"Well, sir – I should ask your wife about that," said the man, shutting his bag with a snap and turning to go. "She'd know. If I may say so, you certainly don't seem well to me. You seem – well – a bit peculiar. Strange, you know. Not at all yourself!"

Twiddle gave such a loud snort that the man fled into the hall in fright and shot out of the front door. *Slam*! He was gone!

"Well, give me my old doctor any day," said Twiddle in disgust. "That one's an idiot. *A-whoooosh-oo*!"

He sat down, and the cat jumped on his knee. He was just snoozing when he heard the front door open and shut. Ah, that was Mrs Twiddle. She came bustling into the room.

"Well, dear, how do you feel? You look better."

"I don't," said Twiddle, gloomily. "The doctor came. He's an ass. He wouldn't even look at my tongue."

"You've been dreaming," said Mrs Twiddle. "You know the doctor hasn't been. He's not coming till half past twelve."

"He has been – black bag and all," said Twiddle, crossly. "He drank some tea and ate some of your cake and said it was good too."

Mrs Twiddle looked at the empty tea-cups and the cut cake in surprise. "*Did* he come?" she said. "Well, well – he said he couldn't arrive till last thing this morning. What did he say about your cold?"

"Nothing. I told you, he wouldn't even look at my tongue," said Twiddle, gloomily. "He didn't look at my throat either – he just measured it very carefully and wrote down something about it in his notebook, but he didn't tell me what it was. And he didn't prescribe me any medicine either. What a doctor! He kept on measuring me – that's about all he

did. Huh! New-fangled, up-to-date ways indeed. Give me old Doctor Brown. At least he knows about throats and tongues and medicines."

"Measuring you!" said Mrs Twiddle, puzzled. "Twiddle, you've been asleep. Oh, yes you have, so don't deny it. Asleep and dreaming! Though why you want to go and dirty two cups and saucers when you got your tea, I don't know."

"I was not asleep and dreaming," said Twiddle, offended. "I tell you that doctor took a tape measure and measured me from head to foot. He must have been quite mad."

Mrs Twiddle sat down in a chair very suddenly and she began to laugh. She laughed till she almost fell off her chair, and the tears ran down her cheeks. Twiddle stared at her in astonishment, and frowned.

"What's so funny about this?" he cried, rapping the table so hard that the cat leaped out of the window. "Sending me a doctor like that! I won't see him again, I tell you that!"

"Twiddle! Oh, Twiddle – you really will be the death of me," gasped Mrs Twiddle. "Have you forgotten that you ordered a new suit?"

"No, of course not. That's nothing to do with it," growled Twiddle.

"But it is," said Mrs Twiddle, wiping away the tears of laughter. "I went to the tailor's this morning, and asked him to send a man to measure you for your new suit as you weren't very well and couldn't come to the shop. They said they'd send a man as soon as they could."

"Good gracious! Was that man who came the tailor's man?" said Twiddle. "I thought he was the doctor. Yes – he had scissors and things in his bag and he kept on and on measuring me. And I kept asking him to look at my tongue and take my temperature! Oh, my dear – he must have thought *I* was mad!"

"He probably did," said Mrs Twiddle and she began to laugh again, quite helplessly. Twiddle got up in disgust. He didn't like being laughed at. "If you don't stop laughing I'll go out and leave you

here alone," he said. But Mrs Twiddle didn't hear him, she was laughing too much. So, when the real doctor came at half past twelve, Twiddle was nowhere to be seen.

"Oh, Doctor – do come in," said Mrs Twiddle. "Now where has Twiddle disappeared to? Twiddle, Twiddle?"

"I heard someone chopping wood in your wood-shed, and whistling loudly," said the doctor. "Would that be your husband? It didn't sound as if there was much the matter with him, Mrs Twiddle."

"Er – well, no – I don't think there is, really," said Mrs Twiddle. "He's just suffered from an attack of muddle-headedness, but I've cured that now, Doctor. I think he must have forgotten that he thought he had a cold!"

Twiddle had forgotten! He had been so angry that he had gone out to chop wood, and now he was feeling happy and good-tempered again. Mrs Twiddle laughed to herself.

"Funny old Twiddle!" she said. "I'll make him his favourite stew for lunch – he'll be so very hungry!"

She was quite right. He was!

Mr Twiddle
and the Boots

Once Mrs Twiddle turned out the landing cupboard, and she found two pairs of Mr Twiddle's old boots. She took them down to the kitchen and looked at them.

"Well, they could really be mended," she said to herself. "They want new soles, but that's all. The heels are quite good, and so are the upper parts. In these hard times we mustn't throw old boots away. I'll tell Twiddle to take them to be soled."

So when Mr Twiddle came in from his walk, he saw the two pairs of old boots on the table. He looked at them in surprise.

"Fancy those old things turning up again!" he said. "I haven't seen them for years."

"They must be soled," said Mrs

Twiddle. "The soles are very bad. Look at them."

"Yes, so they are," said Mr Twiddle, looking at the big holes in the soles. "All right dear – they shall be sold."

Now Twiddle was making a very great mistake. He thought that Mrs Twiddle meant him to sell the boots. When she said they must be soled, he thought she meant sold. She really meant that the soles must be mended, of course – but he didn't know that.

He put the boots into a carrier bag and set off down the road to the shop that

bought old clothes. "I ought to get a nice lot of money for these boots," thought Twiddle, pleased. "What shall I buy with the money? I want a new pipe, really. And Mrs Twiddle could do with some boiled sweets. She does like them so much. And the cat could have a kipper. It has behaved quite well lately."

Mr Twiddle sold the boots and with the money he got, he bought himself a splendid new pipe.

He went to the sweet-shop and bought

a bag of sweets for Mrs Twiddle. And he bought a kipper for the cat, so Twiddle had no money left by the time he got home.

He put down the sweets on the table. Mrs Twiddle was delighted to see them. "Oh, thank you," she said. "That is kind of you. I thought you hadn't any money left this week."

"Well, I've just taken the boots to be sold," said Twiddle. "The man gave me the money."

"But, Twiddle, why did the boot-mender give *you* money?" asked Mrs Twiddle, thinking that the cobbler must have gone mad. After all, she always had to pay money to have her shoes mended – it seemed the wrong way about for the man to pay Twiddle!

"Well, boots that are sold bring in money, don't they?" said Twiddle, thinking that his wife was being very stupid all of a sudden. "Look, I got myself a new pipe, too."

Mrs Twiddle stared at the new pipe. She simply could not understand how it

was that Twiddle had got money for taking boots to be mended!

"And I got a kipper for the cat, too," said Twiddle. "Puss, Puss, Puss!"

The cat jumped up at the kipper. Mrs Twiddle really felt in a whirl … Sweets for her – a pipe for Twiddle – and a kipper for the cat – all because she had sent Twiddle with two pairs of boots to be mended. Well, well, well!

Someone came to the back door just as Mrs Twiddle was going to ask Twiddle a little bit more about it all. When she came back, Twiddle had gone out into the garden, and she forgot all about the affair until three days later.

Then she remembered the boots. She was just going out and she called to Twiddle:

"Twiddle! Look after the kitchen fire for me. I'll be back soon. I'm going to get the groceries, and I shall call at the boot-mender's for your two pairs of boots."

Twiddle stared at his wife in the greatest surprise. "Two pairs of boots!" he said. "That's funny! I've only got two pairs of boots – and one pair is on my feet, and the other is over there waiting to be cleaned."

"I mean the boots that are being mended," said Mrs Twiddle.

"But there aren't any being mended," said Twiddle, wondering if his wife was quite well. "I tell you my boots are on my feet – and over there. Don't be silly, dear."

"Twiddle, I'll thank you not to call me silly," said Mrs Twiddle, offended. "I know what I'm doing. If you've forgotten that there are boots of yours being mended, I haven't!"

She stalked out down the garden path, leaving Twiddle very puzzled. She went to the boot-mender's and asked for Twiddle's boots.

"He brought two pairs here on Monday," she said. "They were to be soled, but not heeled. And by the way, did you give Mr Twiddle money when he brought the boots to you? It seemed such a funny thing to me!"

The cobbler looked in surprise at Mrs Twiddle. "I didn't give Mr Twiddle anything," he said, "and I haven't got his boots either. I don't know what you mean."

"But you must have his boots!" said Mrs Twiddle. "I gave him two old pairs to bring here to be mended. Oh, please, do look for them! Maybe you've forgotten that he brought them."

The cobbler looked all round his shop. There were big boots and little ones there, but not Twiddle's. The cobbler shook his head.

"I'm quite certain that Mr Twiddle didn't bring any boots here," he said.

"He must have taken them to the other cobbler. I feel offended at that, Mrs Twiddle, for you've dealt with me for years!"

He bent over his work, quite angry. Mrs Twiddle blushed, for she hated anyone to be angry with her. She went out of the shop, furious with Twiddle, because she thought he had gone with his boots to the other cobbler's and hadn't

141

told her. She hurried home as fast as she could go.

"Twiddle!" she cried, bursting into the kitchen. "Twiddle! Why did you take your boots to the other cobbler on Monday, instead of to the one we always go to? Now you just tell me that!"

Twiddle really thought his wife had gone mad. Here she was talking about boots again! He thought he had better get her to bed and fetch the doctor. So he put his arm round her and tried to get her to the stairs. Mrs Twiddle was really angry.

"Twiddle! Let go of my arm! What do you mean by saying I must go to bed and see the doctor? It's you who ought to do that! You're losing your memory. You've forgotten already that you took those old pairs of boots to be soled on Monday!"

"Dear me, I haven't forgotten that," said Twiddle, suddenly remembering. "I told you I'd taken them, didn't I? And I bought you some boiled sweets out of the money that the man gave me."

"He didn't give you any money!" cried

142

poor Mrs Twiddle. "He says he didn't. I asked him. Why do you tell me dreadful stories like that, Twiddle? To think we have been married for thirty years and now you are beginning to tell me stories."

"I tell you, dear, I took those boots to the old-clothes shop, and I sold them, just as you told me to," said Twiddle, quite in despair. "I don't know why the man said he didn't give me any money, but he did, and I spent it all."

Mrs Twiddle stared at Twiddle, and suddenly she knew what had happened.

She gave a groan that startled Twiddle very much.

"Oh, foolish man! Oh, stupid, ridiculous man! Oh, silly, silly man! I told you those boots were to be soled – s-o-l-e-d, Twiddle – and you went and sold them – s-o-l-d. I wanted you to get new soles put on them – and you go and sell them! Twiddle, will you ever, ever do anything really sensible? No – you never will!"

Grumbling Grace

Do you know anyone who grumbles? I know plenty of people!

When it rains they say, "Oh dear! How I wish it wouldn't rain!" And when the sun shines they say, "What a nuisance, it's so hot today!"

The grumblers are very tiresome and the funny thing is, they always begin when they are children. I am sure you know a few grumblers – maybe you are one yourself, though I hope not!

This is the tale of grumbling Grace, and how her mother cured her.

Grace was nine years old, and she had grumbled about things ever since she could speak. So she was a marvellous grumbler by the time she was nine.

She grumbled about getting up. She

grumbled about going to bed. She grumbled because there was ginger cake for tea instead of chocolate cake. And when there was chocolate cake she grumbled because there wasn't ginger!

She grumbled because she wasn't at the top of her class. She grumbled because she didn't get a prize. She grumbled because Jenny had a new dress and she hadn't, and she grumbled because John had a bigger pencil-box than she had.

So, as you can imagine, she was grumbling all day long! Her mother was so used to it that she didn't notice it – and it wasn't until her Aunt Joan came to stay for a few days that anyone tried to stop Grace from grumbling.

"Goodness me! How that child grumbles!" cried Aunt Joan. "I never heard anything like it. Why don't you stop her?"

"Well, really, I haven't noticed it," said Grace's mother, in surprise. "I suppose Grace has done it for so long that I am used to it and don't bother."

"Well, my dear, you must bother," said Aunt Joan firmly. "That child will grow up into a most unpleasant woman. When she marries she will grumble at her poor husband and children. No one will love her. You really must cure her, or she will be unhappy when she grows up."

"Yes – I suppose I must," said Grace's mother. "I'll think of some way to cure her. I don't think Grace herself knows how she grumbles."

"I'm sure she doesn't," said Aunt Joan.

"She can't open her mouth without grumbling, poor child. She wastes such a lot of breath! No wonder she isn't top of her class. No wonder children don't ask her out to tea. No wonder she always looks miserable and discontented! Grumblers are always like that."

Aunt Joan left soon after that. Grace was glad. She hadn't dared to grumble quite so much when her aunt was there, because Aunt Joan always noticed a grumble, and her mother didn't. But now Mother was going to notice too!

"Grace, your Aunt Joan was quite right," said Mother. "I have counted your grumbles today and there have already been sixteen!"

"Oh no, Mummy, surely not," said Grace, going red. "I don't really grumble, you know, really I don't."

"Well, we'll see what your next grumble is," said her mother. "And if you can't stop grumbling, we'll make some plan that will show you exactly how much or how little you do grumble!"

Well, five minutes later Grace began to

grumble, of course. She had a beautiful little bedroom of her own, with a nice white chest-of-drawers, a comfortable little bed, two green rugs, a bookcase, a chair, and a mirror with flowers round it, a clock, and a stool.

And will you believe it, she began to grumble about her bedroom. She was talking about Jane and Rosie, who were sisters and shared a room together.

"I do wish I had a sister," she said. "It's so dull alone. Rosie and Jane share a room together. I don't like having a bedroom all to myself. I wish I could share it with someone."

"Oh, Grace! You have such a beautiful little bedroom!" said her mother, vexed. "I tried to make it so nice for you!"

"Well, it's not so nice as Rosie and Jane's," said Grace in her usual grumbling tone.

"Now, Grace – this is a great big grumble," said her mother. "And it's told me what to do with you to show you how much and how often you grumble. Listen! Every time you grumble I shall go to your nice little bedroom and take something out of it. If you grumble at your bedroom you don't deserve to have so many nice things in it and you will lose them one by one!"

Grace stared at her mother in dismay. "No, please don't do that, Mummy," she said. "I shouldn't like it at all. And anyway, it wouldn't be any good because I don't really grumble as much as Aunt Joan said I did."

"Well, we'll see," said her mother.

"Now remember, Grace – every grumble loses you something out of your bedroom!"

Grace thought it was a silly idea. She didn't say anything for a long time. She remembered not to grumble and her mother was pleased. But after lunch, when her mother told her to take a book and rest until school-time, she was cross.

"I don't see why I can't go into the garden," she grumbled. "I wish I..."

Her mother looked at Grace – and then she ran upstairs. She took the stool out of the bedroom and put it into the spare

room. Grace missed it when she went to brush her hair. Bother! She liked that little stool.

She went downstairs and began to grumble again. "Mummy, I do wish you hadn't taken that stool," she began. "I do think it's…"

Her mother went upstairs again. This time she took out the chair. Now Grace had nowhere to sit!

Grace went to school, sulking. When she came home she wondered what jam there was for tea. She lifted up the lid of the jam-pot.

"Oh, plum jam," she grumbled. "Mummy, why couldn't I have strawberry jam? I do wish…"

Her mother slipped upstairs at once and took away the clock from Grace's bedroom. Grace felt cross. She sat down to tea and spread some plum jam on her bread-and-butter.

"How did you get on at school this afternoon, Grace?" asked her mother.

"Well, I would have done my writing nicely if only John hadn't jogged my

arm," grumbled Grace. "And we had such a lot of arithmetic, Mummy. I think we have too much. I wish…"

Her mother left the table as soon as Grace began grumbling and went upstairs. She moved the dressing-table out of the room! Good gracious – the room began to look very bare indeed.

Grace didn't stop grumbling. She grumbled because it was raining and she couldn't go out after tea. She grumbled because she had some spelling to learn. She grumbled because her mother sent her to wash her jammy hands.

And every time she grumbled her mother went upstairs and took something out of Grace's little bedroom. Her mirror went. Her pictures went. Her bookcase full of books went – and her two green rugs! Would you believe that anyone could grumble quite so much? It was simply astonishing.

"Well, I had no idea that Grace was such a terrible grumbler!" thought her mother sadly. "How wrong I have been to let her get so bad. I am afraid it is going to be very difficult to cure her after all these years."

Grace went up to her room to fetch a book. She opened the door – and then stood staring in alarm and surprise. Only her bed was left in the room! There was nothing else at all – no chair, no rugs on the floor, no pictures on the wall! It was dreadful!

"Mummy! What have you done with all my things?" cried Grace. "There's only the bed left!"

"Yes – isn't it shocking, Grace?" said her mother. "You have grumbled almost

every time you opened your mouth and I have had to go upstairs very often and take something away. Now for goodness sake don't make one single grumble more, or your bed will go! And you don't want to sleep on the floor, do you?"

"No," said Grace, in horror. Goodness! Had she really grumbled so much as to lose everything but her bed? She must be very, very bad. Well, she wasn't going to lose her bed – she wouldn't grumble once more that night.

And she didn't. Not once. It showed that she could stop herself if she liked. Her mother smiled a little secret smile and was pleased. Grace would learn to stop grumbling sooner that she had hoped.

The next day Grace's mother spoke to her at breakfast-time. "Today, Grace, you will lose a toy for every grumble. Now it isn't very nice to have a bedroom with only a bed in it, is it? Well, it will not be at all nice to have a toy-cupboard with not a single toy in. So be careful, won't you?"

"Oh, Mummy! It isn't fair!" cried Grace. "I do wish..."

"There goes your first doll, Grace," said her mother, and she got up from the table. "That was a grumble, you know. Now do be careful."

It was Saturday and Grace was at home all day. She was cross. She was sulky. She grumbled without ceasing, and very soon she had lost her monkey, three dolls, her jigsaw puzzle, four books, her teddy-bear, and her teaset. It was dreadful!

"You know, Grace, I thought last night you would soon learn not to grumble," said her mother sadly. "But I was wrong. You are worse than ever today."

"Only because I am cross, so I'm not trying," said Grace. "If I tried I wouldn't grumble once!"

"I don't believe that," said her mother. So Grace set out to show her mother that what she said was true. And until bedtime came the little girl did not grumble once! It was so nice to be with her – she was cheerful and merry, and her mother hardly knew her.

"Grace! If only you knew how sweet you are when you don't grumble!" cried her mother. "I love you ten times more!"

"Well – I like myself much better too," said Grace, astonished that she felt so happy. "Mummy, give me back my toys and my bedroom things. I won't grumble any more. I promise!"

"Very well. I'll believe you and trust you," said her mother. She put back all the bedroom things and all the toys. Grace was very happy.

And now, does she grumble? Never! It was such a shock to lose all her things that it really did show her what a grumbler she was. I hope your mother doesn't try the same trick with you, if you grumble! I shouldn't like to hear that you had to sleep on the floor.

Mr Twiddle and the
Dog Tinker

"Twiddle! Where are you, Twiddle? Do come and see what I've got!" called Mrs Twiddle, hurrying into the house.

Twiddle looked round as his happy little wife came into the room. A small brown dog trotted beside her, his tongue hanging out, looking very pleased with himself.

The cat, asleep on the hearth-rug, woke up at once, spat fiercely at the surprised dog and leaped straight out of the window.

"A dog!" said Twiddle, amazed. "Surely you haven't bought a dog, my dear! You always say you don't like them because they have muddy paws and leave hairs all over the place."

"But this one is sweet!" said Mrs

Twiddle, and patted its brown head. "I haven't bought it, Twiddle – it belongs to old Mrs Lanton down the road, and she's going away so she begged me to have the dog for a day or two."

"I see," said Twiddle, quite relived. "Well, there's one good thing about having a dog – the cat will keep nicely out of the way! I've fallen over it twice already this morning. Did you see how it shot out of the window when it saw the dog? Ha, ha – that was funny!"

"Oh dear, I forgot that my poor Puss wouldn't like a dog," said Mrs Twiddle, looking worried. "Perhaps I'd better take it back."

"No, don't. It's rather a nice dog," said Twiddle. "And if it will keep that cat away, I'll be delighted. What's its name?"

"Tinker," said Mrs Twiddle. "Would you like a bone, Tinker? Bone?"

"Wuff!" said Tinker joyfully, and leaped happily round Mrs Twiddle. It then ran between Twiddle's legs, and made him sit down rather suddenly. Luckily there was a chair just behind him.

"Isn't he playful?" said Mrs Twiddle. "Look at him jumping up at you, Twiddle. He likes you!"

The little dog leaped up on Twiddle's knee, planted his front paws on his chest, and licked his nose lovingly. Twiddle didn't like it. He put the dog down firmly, and took out his handkerchief to dry his licked nose.

"Wuff!" said the dog joyfully, and snatched it out of his hand and ran off with it.

162

Twiddle began to think that dogs were worse than cats. "Bring that back!" he roared.

And to his great surprise, the dog brought the handkerchief and dropped it neatly at his feet.

"There now!" said Mrs Twiddle. "See how obedient he is." But as soon as Twiddle bent down to pick up the handkerchief, the dog was off and away with it again! Oh dear – life was going to be difficult, living with that dog, Twiddle thought!

Still, there was one good thing – the cat didn't show its nose all day long! Twiddle was pleased. The dog was more polite than the cat, too – it didn't sit and glare at him rudely, and it did come when it was called, and that was a thing the cat never did!

All the same, Twiddle was very tired of the dog by the time evening came. He found it very uncomfortable to walk down the garden with Tinker racing round and round his legs. "And why you think you've got to bark madly every time I come into the room, I don't know," said Twiddle. "You'll end in making me deaf!"

The dog was very, very anxious to please Mr and Mrs Twiddle. He brought in the most peculiar-smelling things from the rubbish heap and laid them gently at their feet as if he were bringing them wonderful gifts. Mrs Twiddle pretended to be pleased, so as not to upset him, and patted him lovingly.

But Twiddle didn't like these gifts at all. "What's this he's brought in now?"

he said in disgust, as the dog draped the remains of a very old smelly kipper across his feet. "Look here, wife – I won't have this kind of thing! Pooh – what a smell. Take it away, you silly dog! Pooh!"

The dog took it away sorrowfully, his tail well down. Twiddle felt as if he had been very cruel – but really he was not going to have half his rubbish heap piled on his feet all day long! He settled back in his chair and began to read his paper, and his wife sat down to do some mending.

"Twiddle – I'm afraid you'll have to go and change your slippers," said Mrs Twiddle after a while. "I can still smell that kippery smell."

"I am not going to change my slippers," said Twiddle. "Can't I have some peace?" But after a while the smell of the kipper was so strong that he got up, grumbling, shook off his slippers in the kitchen, and put on some others. Then he sat down again.

"Twiddle – I think you ought to change your socks, too," said Mrs Twiddle after a bit. "I can still smell that smell."

"Are you going to make me change all

my clothes one by one?" demanded Twiddle fiercely. "I don't care if my socks do smell of kipper – here I sit and here I stay."

All the same, the smell was really dreadful. Soon Twiddle got up with a groan and went to change his socks. But no sooner had he sat down than his wife began to sniff again.

"I can still smell that smell," she said. "It comes from somewhere in your direction, Twiddle, it really does."

Twiddle couldn't help thinking that it did too. He got up and looked all around. "Perhaps the dog hid that horrible kipper somewhere in the room," he said, and went round sniffing as if he were a dog himself.

Mrs Twiddle got up to sniff round, too, and soon her nose took her straight to Twiddle's chair – and there, behind his cushion, were hidden the remains of that dreadful old kipper!

"So I changed my shoes and socks all for nothing!" said Twiddle. "The smell's behind the cushion! Where's that dog?

I'll give him such a smacking!"

But Mrs Twiddle wouldn't let him. She took off the cushion-cover and went to wash it. The dog followed her excitedly – what a lovely smell of kipper!

On the second night that the dog stayed with them, Mrs Twiddle went out to a meeting. "I can't take the dog," she said to Twiddle. "I'll leave him with you. He'll be quite all right if you let him lie beside you on the rug. And don't listen to him if he whines for his dinner – he's just had it."

"I won't," said Twiddle grimly. "He's too fat as it is. Not a crumb will I give him!"

Mrs Twiddle went out and the front door banged. Twiddle settled down happily in front of the fire, and Tinker sat with his head on Twiddle's knee, looking at him so lovingly that Twiddle felt quite uncomfortable.

"Don't stare so," he said to the dog. "It's bad manners." But the dog went on staring, so Twiddle had to put up with it.

Soon the fire died down and Twiddle
gave a groan. "Now I've got to go out to
the wood-shed and get some logs – and
it's dark. Oh well, the fire will go out if I
don't fetch them! Stay here, Tinker."

He left Tinker on the rug, and went
out of the back door to the wood-shed. He
brought back six good logs and put one
on the fire. Then he sat down to read
again. He suddenly remembered the dog.

"Tinker! Where are you?" he called.
"Blow the dog – he must have gone

upstairs. I hope he isn't lying on the bed!
Well – he knows his way downstairs, so
I'm not going all the way up to get him."

Twiddle soon fell asleep. When he
woke up the dog still wasn't there, and
Twiddle began to feel worried.

He hunted all over the house for him.
No dog anywhere!

"Good gracious – he must have slipped
out when I went for the logs!" said
Twiddle. "Whatever will my wife say
when she comes back and finds him
gone? Bother that dog – I'll have to go
out and look for him!"

So he went out and began to call the
dog. "Tinker, Tinker, Tinker! Good dog,
then! Come along, Tinker, come along!"
But no Tinker came. Twiddle felt more
and more worried.

He put his coat on and went down the
road. He called and called. "Tinker! Come
along, then. Dinner, dinner! Boney,
boney! Good dog, Tinker!"

And then, what a relief! There came a
little bark, and a dog raced up to Twiddle
and licked his hand. Twiddle was so glad

that he picked him up and hugged him. "I shall carry you all the way home, then you can't run away again," he said.

So home he went with the dog, and gave him a big piece of meat-pie. The dog seemed very hungry indeed. He was just licking the last crumb off the plate when the front door opened and in came little Mrs Twiddle. Twiddle went out to the hall to help her off with her coat.

"How's the little dog?" said Mrs Twiddle. "Has he been good?"

"Oh very!" said Twiddle. "Good as

gold. Er – I gave him a little snack, dear, he seemed so—"

"Twiddle – you didn't give him any of that meat-pie, did you?" said Mrs Twiddle, frowning.

"Well," said Twiddle, following her into the kitchen, "well, you see …"

And then Mrs Twiddle stopped and stared as if she couldn't believe her eyes. She stared first at the dog and then at Twiddle, looking so astounded that Twiddle felt quite scared.

"What's the matter?" he said.

"Look – the dog's different!" said Mrs Twiddle. "It's black, not brown. And it's got a short tail, not a long one. What a very peculiar thing. Surely the dog was brown before, surely it had—"

Just then a truly awful thought struck Twiddle. He stared at the dog, too. Yes – it was quite different from Tinker. Quite! He had brought in someone else's dog from the road! Oh, what a thing to do! Then where was Tinker?

"You're not Tinker, are you?" said Mrs Twiddle to the dog. But to her surprise it

leaped up and licked her. She bent down and looked at its collar. "It says 'Tinker, White House'," she said. "But our Tinker came from Redroofs, where old Mrs Lanton lives. What's the meaning of this, Twiddle? Please explain!"

Twiddle groaned. "I couldn't find Tinker and went out into the road, calling him," he said. "And this dog ran up to me. How was I to know there were two dogs called Tinker?"

"But didn't you even notice that it was a different dog?" asked Mrs Twiddle.

"Twiddle, what is the matter with your brains? Oh, how I wish I could go and buy you some really good ones! Really – the things you do! And now, the thing is, where's our Tinker? Did you let him out?"

"He must have slipped out when I fetched the logs," said Twiddle. "He may be in the wood-shed. I'll go and see."

Then off went Twiddle out of the back-door to the wood-shed, and there, fast asleep and looking very comfortable indeed on a couple of soft sacks, was Tinker! He didn't even open one eye or prick an ear when Twiddle looked in. Twiddle shut the door softly.

"You can sleep there for the night, Tinker," he said. "You're safe there – and I'd like a little peace from both you and the cat. Oh, to sit in my chair without either of you pestering me!"

He went back indoors. "It's all right, my dear," he said. "Tinker's asleep in the shed. I hadn't the heart to wake him, he looked so comfortable – and really it would be nice to have a quiet evening

without a cat or dog in the house!"

"The cat came in the kitchen door," said Mrs Twiddle. "It smelled the smell of kipper in your... oh Twiddle, be careful – it's there, in your chair!"

But Twiddle was already sitting in his chair with a look of great surprise on his face. He had sat on the cat! She yowled and put out her claws – and Twiddle yelled and leaped out of his chair as if a bomb had gone off beneath him!

Mrs Twiddle laughed until the tears ran down her cheeks in streams. She laughed so much that Twiddle got cross, and went straight to bed, very upset indeed. That dog – that cat! Why couldn't animals leave him alone?

He fell asleep – but Twiddle, you're soon going to wake up, I'm afraid! Tinker will feel lonely, and he'll whine miserably out in the shed – and who will have to fetch him into the house? You will, Twiddle – what a shame!

Mr Twiddle
and the Toothpaste

Mr Twiddle cleaned his teeth well every night and morning. He had a blue toothbrush, and Mrs Twiddle had a yellow one.

Mr Twiddle liked toothpaste in a tube and Mrs Twiddle liked it in a tin. So they couldn't possibly mistake each other's brushes or toothpaste when they cleaned their teeth.

Now one night Mr Twiddle found that he had squeezed every scrap of toothpaste out of his tube. So he called to his wife from the bathroom:

"My love! Will you get me some more toothpaste tomorrow? Mine's finished."

"I don't see why you can't remember to get it yourself," said Mrs Twiddle. "You pass the chemist's each morning when you fetch the paper."

"Well, I will get it then," said Mr Twiddle.

"You'll never remember," said Mrs Twiddle. "I know you, Twiddle! If you had to get your own toothpaste you'd never have any to clean your teeth with for the rest of your life."

"What an untruthful thing to say!" said Twiddle, feeling quite cross, especially as he knew it was very likely true. He did have a very bad memory. "A most untruthful and ridiculous thing to say. I shall buy some tomorrow."

But he didn't buy any. He passed the chemist's on his way to fetch the paper, but he didn't think about toothpaste at all, although one side of the window was filled with nothing but different kinds of toothpaste!

So, that night, he again took up the empty tube and squeezed it. "Bother!" he thought. "I didn't get the toothpaste! Well, I shan't say a word."

He didn't. But Mrs Twiddle did. "I hope your new toothpaste is all right," she called slyly, knowing perfectly well that Twiddle hadn't bought any.

"I am going to buy some tomorrow," said Twiddle in rather a high-and-mighty voice.

He went to get his paper as usual the next day, and when he came to the chemist's he stopped.

"Now, what was I going to buy here?" he wondered. "What was I going to buy? Razor-blades? A bottle of cough mixture? Some blackcurrant lozenges?"

He went in and bought all of them,

thinking that one of them must be right. Mrs Twiddle smiled to herself when she saw what he had bought.

"You've decided not to clean your teeth with toothpaste after all!" she said, in a polite sort of voice. "I see you have been to the chemist's and bought quite a lot of things, but not any toothpaste."

Twiddle felt so angry with himself that he nearly boxed his own ears. He went very red and Mrs Twiddle laughed.

"I'll buy some for you myself this afternoon," she said. So she did, because she had a very good memory, and hardly ever forgot to do what she said she would.

She came in at teatime with her shopping in a basket. She went to put the kettle on and then she unpacked her shopping.

"There's your toothpaste," she said, picking up a long tube. "And here are some buns for tea. And here's a new pair of brown laces for you – and please put them into your brown shoes, not your black ones – and here's some glue to

180

mend that broken teapot spout – and
here's a new book from the library – and
I've remembered to get you the soap you
like."

"Thank you, my love," said Twiddle,
wishing he had as good a memory as his
wife had.

"Now do take the things that belong to
you and put them away," said Mrs
Twiddle.

But, of course, Twiddle didn't. He left
the laces and everything else on the side-
table, and Mrs Twiddle felt quite
impatient when she saw them there.

"Now he'll forget where he put the laces and the toothpaste," she thought. "Well, well, I shan't put the laces in his shoes for him and I shan't take his toothpaste upstairs. He really must learn to do little things for himself."

So, when Twiddle came to do his teeth again that night, once more he found that all he had on the shelf was an empty tube, quite squeezed out.

"Now let me think," he said to himself. "Just let me think. I *have* got some toothpaste now. Mrs Twiddle got it for me. It isn't here. So it must still be downstairs on the little table. I'll go and get it before she asks me if I've cleaned my teeth."

So Mr Twiddle crept downstairs in the dark, went to the little table in the kitchen and groped about for the toothpaste tube.

Soon he went upstairs again, very quietly, holding a tube in his hand. He didn't know he had the tube of glue instead of the tube of toothpaste. He had quite forgotten that Mrs Twiddle had bought him some glue to mend the old teapot for her.

"Twiddle! Are you cleaning your teeth properly tonight?" called Mrs Twiddle from the bedroom.

"Yes, dear, of course!" answered Twiddle, taking off the top of the tube of glue and squeezing some glue on to his toothbrush.

"Funny colour!" he thought, when he

saw it. "Not the same as usual. And what a nasty fishy smell! I wish I had gone to buy the toothpaste myself. Mrs Twiddle hasn't bought the kind I usually have."

He began to rub his teeth with it. Oh, what a dreadful taste! Twiddle couldn't bear it. He tried to open his teeth to rinse his mouth with water. But to his amazement and horror he couldn't get his teeth apart. No wonder, because the glue was sticking them fast together!

"Twiddle! Aren't you ever coming to bed?" called Mrs Twiddle, impatiently.

"Ooogle-oo-oo," said Twiddle, trying to say "Just coming!" His lips seemed to be sticking together now, too. Whatever could be the matter?

"What did you say, Twiddle?" called Mrs Twiddle, astonished.

"Ug-ug-ug-ug," answered Twiddle, feeling really alarmed now.

"Twiddle! Speak up! Don't mumble like that," said Mrs Twiddle, sharply.

"Oooph, oooph, ug," said Twiddle, and looked at himself in the mirror in fright. Why couldn't he talk? Why couldn't he open his mouth? Whatever was happening?

"Do you think you're being funny, Twiddle?" cried Mrs Twiddle, beginning to get cross.

Twiddle didn't think he was being funny at all, but he did think he was being very strange. He worked his lips about, trying to open them. But they were stuck fast.

Mrs Twiddle jumped out of bed. She

wasn't going to let Twiddle behave like that to her, mumbling and muttering instead of giving her a proper answer. She came sailing in to the bathroom in her dressing-gown, looking so furious that Twiddle felt quite frightened.

"Twiddle! What is the matter with you? Answer me at once!" said Mrs Twiddle.

But that was more than poor Twiddle could do. He stared forlornly at Mrs Twiddle, and then tried to open his mouth by pulling at his stuck-together lips with his fingers, making a curious gurgling noise as he did so.

"The man's gone mad!" said Mrs Twiddle in fright. "Oh dear, I'd better get the doctor!"

But before she went to get him she had a look round the bathroom, and there, on the shelf, lay the tube of glue, a little golden drop oozing out of the tip. Mrs Twiddle picked it up and looked at it. Then she looked at Twiddle. Then she picked up his toothbrush and felt it. The bristles stuck to her fingers!

"Twiddle," said Mrs Twiddle. "Oh, Twiddle! First you can't remember to buy yourself toothpaste – then I buy it for you – and yet you go and clean your teeth with the glue I bought to mend the teapot spout. Twiddle, are you mad or just plain silly? What am I to do with you?"

Twiddle stared at the tube of glue in horror. His eyes looked ready to drop out of his head. So that was why it smelled so fishy. Good gracious, he had stuck his teeth and lips together and perhaps he would never be able to get them unstuck again. Mrs Twiddle always bought such strong glue!

"You'd better come to bed before you do anything else silly," said Mrs Twiddle. "Come along. You'll be washing your face with the toothpaste and brushing your hair with the bathroom stool if I leave you for a moment!"

Mr Twiddle got into bed, very sad and very much alarmed. It was awful to have to listen and listen to Mrs Twiddle and not be able to answer back at all. He felt so bad about it after half an hour of listening that some big tears rolled down his cheeks.

And there must have been something very strong in poor Mr Twiddle's tears, because the drops unstuck the glue on his

lips and teeth, and he was able to open
his mouth again and speak! Oh, how glad
he was. He sat up in bed and opened and
shut his mouth like a goldfish.

"Oooph!" said Twiddle, finding his
voice again. "One more word from you
Mrs Twiddle, and I get the glue and stick
your lips together. Just one more word!"

And Mrs Twiddle was so astonished
to hear Twiddle talk to her like that that
she didn't say another word; so Twiddle
was able to go peacefully to sleep after he
had washed his lips and teeth well to get
rid of the taste of glue.

But Mrs Twiddle did have the last word, of course, the next day. She gave Twiddle the teapot to mend and handed him two tubes, the tube of toothpaste and the tube of glue.

"You probably want to use your toothpaste instead of the glue to stick on the spout," she said, in a polite voice. "So here are both. Use which you like."

And that annoyed Twiddle so much that he actually thought about what he was doing, and mended the spout really well, with the glue!